The Embassy

Amber Lewis

The Embassy

Copyright © 2011 by Amber Lewis

ISBN 1467936065

www.amazon.com

Acknowledgments

Special thanks to all my friends and family who continue to support me in all my endeavors.

Book Editor: Michael Valentino

Co-Editor: Amber Lewis

Interior Illustration: Various

Cover Design: Touchables Typesetting

 Interior Design and Typesetting: Touchables
Typesetting

Table of Contents

Eyes of the Beholder

Life in the little town of Collinsville was peaceful. Typical small town, everyone knew each other and things were simple. There wasn't the hustle and bustle of city life. Day to day living was generally calm and quiet. Johnny loved the serenity of the country lifestyle. He dreamed of one day marrying and raising a family in his tranquil little town. Crime was low, businesses were thriving and the residents never failed to come to each other's aide.

Amber Lewis

Johnny awakened feeling fresh and alive. He pulled his bedroom curtains back. A bright burst of sunlight filled his bedroom. He gazed out at the clear blue skies. With a jovial smile, he glanced about his backyard noting the leaves on the trees were just starting to change colors. He stretched out his tired arms and headed for the shower.

Before long, he was out the door and strolling through the park enjoying the perfect autumn day. There was a sense of vitality flowing through him. He sucked in the cool fall air and released it without losing his carefree smile. He took a short break and sat down on the wooden bench. He continued to look around in awe at nature's beauty. He had spent his whole life in the small town of Collinsville and was eager to give back to his community. Visions of finishing college and starting up a law firm, in his little town, filled his mind. Although money was tight, he believed he had found a source to help alleviate some of the financial burden.

Johnny thought back to the day he walked down the university hall and saw an advertisement pinned on a clipboard. The ad requested volunteers for an experimental project. Desperate for money, he jotted down the information from the ad and rushed home. He did not waste anytime picking up the telephone to speak with the person in charge. He was directed to Doctor Gunter.

The doctor quickly explained, "I am developing a drug that will give you more energy and increase your memory."

Once the doctor finished providing Johnny with all the details, Johnny saw nothing wrong with volunteering for what appeared to be a harmless experiment. Johnny scheduled his appointment and eagerly waited for the day to come when he could make a few extra bucks to help with his college expenses. Now the day was here and he was more than ready to take whatever test he needed in order to advance his career goals. Hopeful, he continued on his walk to the clinic.

Paid in Full

Johnny had been in the volunteer program for three months and was anxious for the exercise to be over. He had seen more needles in three months than he has seen in his twenty-two years of living. He swiped his pass card and hurriedly entered the medical facility. As usual, Officer Stein paced up and down the hallway. Johnny always felt uneasy by the sight of Officer Stein's gun and military uniform. Nevertheless, he smiled politely, nodded his head and headed to Doctor Gunter's office. He lightly tapped on the door.

"Come in," Gunter shouted.

Johnny's spirits were high because he knew the testing was near an end. He stuck his head inside the room. "Is it okay that I'm early?" he asked.

Gunter was excited to see him. He fanned his hand for him to enter. Gunter twirled the green colored chemicals around in the clear bottle. His grin was wide. "I am just about finished. Please, sit down."

Paid in Full

Johnny took a seat on the medical exam table. There was a clear tone of relief in Johnny's voice when he commented, "So, doc, this is it?"

"Yes, Johnny. Just one more injection and this will all be over." Gunter approached him with a hypodermic needle.

Johnny rolled up his sleeve. He grimaced before the needle went in.

Gunter chuckled. "I would have thought you would be used to this by now."

"Can't say that I am." Johnny squinted with pain as Gunter stuck the needle into his arm. Johnny was thankful that he had received his final inoculation. His arm was sore from the injection. He rolled down his sleeve. Grateful the experiment was near an end, he said, "No offense, Doc, but I'm glad this is almost over."

Dr. Gunter grinned and held out Johnny's reward for completing the testing. "Here's your check."

Johnny happily reached out his hand and took the payment. He looked at all the zeros and was thrilled. "Hey, this is much more than we agreed on."

"You earned it. You were the only one, out of my six patients, who completed the program." Dr. Gunter was wearing a mischievous grin. "Just consider it a bonus."

Johnny smiled. "Thanks, Doc."

"Just don't forget what I said, this is strictly confidential. No one is to know about this," Gunter reminded him.

"Got it," Johnny said.

"And Johnny, don't forget that I need to see you by the end of the week."

"I'll be here." Johnny stepped down from the medical exam table. He grabbed his jacket from the chair and placed his big, fat check into his blue jeans pants pocket. "See you, Doc."

Doctor Gunter patted Johnny on the back, "See you, Johnny."

—

Johnny was floating on air. He was thrilled with the extra bucks Doctor Gunter rewarded him. He even contemplated quitting his job at the hotel. After three years of serving as a cook, he had just about enough of his cruel boss. When he reached the Embassy Hotel, high spirited, he entered the kitchen. It was obvious from the jovial look upon his face that something was up.

"You're late," his boss yelled.

Johnny lied through his teeth. "Sorry, I overslept."

Callously, his boss grunted, "I'm not interested in your excuses. Just get to work."

Johnny sneered at him. He hated his boss. Johnny walked away and pulled out several pots and pans.

"God, what an asshole!" Brian said, once their boss left the kitchen.

Johnny did not get as upset as he usually did. He continued to think about the large check he had in his pants pocket.

"I have a good mind to quit," Johnny remarked.

"Come on, Johnny. If you quit, how are you going to pay for school?"

"I have options," Johnny said.

Brian looked sneaky. His voice was low, "Don't tell me. You were late because you were out on a job interview?"

"Something like that," Johnny said.

Paid in Full

"I hope you get it. I don't blame you for wanting to leave this place. Paul can be a real jerk."

Johnny turned around and began to prepare the soup of the day.

Time Off

Wes yelled toward the bathroom at his wife. "Hurry up; we are going to be late."

"I'm almost ready," Shari shouted back.

Wes turned around in frustration. He took a sip of his cold beer. "Women, they are so freaking slow," he muttered.

"I heard that," Shari yelled out from the bathroom.

Wes checked out the time on his watch. Exasperated, he said, "Come on, kids, let's put these bags in the car. Maybe by the time we're done, your mother will have finished putting on her makeup."

Wes and his two kids loaded up the mini-van with their luggage. All were eager and excited about spending the weekend in the country. Finally as they loaded the last bag into the hatchback, Shari came running from out the house.

Wes had to admit that she was well worth the wait. She looked fabulous in her white cotton blouse and green flowered skirt. He especially loved it when she pinned her hair up in a ponytail. It reminded him of when they first met.

He smiled with pleasure. "It's about time."

She remarked, "A girl has to look her best."

He complimented her, "And that you do."

He patted her on the butt as she walked past him. She giggled like a schoolgirl. Within minutes, the four were off for a week-end getaway.

—

After being in the car for nearly two hours, Kyle impatiently asked, "Are we there yet?"

"We will be there within the hour," Wes informed him.

Shari continued to gaze out the window in awe of the beautiful scenery. She loved how colorful the leaves on the trees were. The further they drove into the country the quieter everything became. It was so peaceful and serene. It was a far cry different from their noisy city life.

Wes looked over at her, "What are you smiling about?" he asked.

Shari turned to face him, her face wreathed in tranquility. "This is wonderful. I'm happy you decided to take some time off work and spend it with us." She sighed with relaxation. "It's nice to be out in the open country away from all the noise and crowds."

Wes grinned. "Anything for you, baby."

Again, Kyle wanted to know, "Are we there yet?"

Slightly annoyed from his son's pestering, Wes verbally snapped, "Please, stop asking me that. When we get there, you will know. Now sit back and be quiet."

Kyle sat back and put on his headphones.

"He's just excited, honey."

Wes tone was a bit calmer. "I know."

Shari turned her head to gaze out the window and resumed her nature watching.

—

Time Off

Wes and his family had finally arrived at the quaint hotel. They all eagerly got out of the van. Wes opened the double doors of the hotel for his family and briskly walked up to the check-in counter.

"Can I help you?" the beautiful blonde asked him.

"Yes, I have reservations for Wes Brown."

She typed his name in the computer. She smiled and handed him his key card. "Here, you are, Mr. Brown. You are in room 452." She pointed her long fingernail. "Just take the elevators to your left. I hope you enjoy your stay."

Wes grinned politely, "Thank you."

Once he received his key-card, Kyle, quickly snatched it from his hand. He and his sister, Alyssa, rushed toward the elevator.

"Don't run," Shari yelled out to them.

Wes looked at Shari and said, "I hope you didn't forget anything like last time because we are way too far out to go back home."

She presented him with a naughty little grin and said, "Don't worry, honey, I packed everything I need." Shari looked all about the hotel. She loved the array of colorful water fountains. The well maintained green plants were a nice touch. She thought *'God, I wish my plants at home looked like these.'* "This is a pretty nice place," she commented.

Wes was pleased that his wife was happy. Proudly, he said, "Only the best for you, baby."

The four entered the elevator and got off on the fourth floor. Kyle and Alyssa raced to the room. As soon as they entered, the kids put down their bags and began jumping up and down on the beds.

"Hey, stop that," Wes ordered.

"Can we go swimming?" Alyssa asked.

Shari presented the children with a demure smile and said, "Sure, you guys go ahead."

Alyssa hurriedly grabbed her bag and rushed to the bathroom to change into her swimsuit. Kyle stood at the bathroom door. He chose to be a nuisance. He kept tapping on the door. "Come on, hurry up in there."

Time Off

Wes and Shari gleamed at each other. They were anxious for the kids to leave. The idea of spending a little quiet time alone was very appealing. Within minutes, the kids were dressed in their swimsuits and out the door. Wes instantly reached out and grabbed Shari into his arms. He could not wait to feel her soft lips pressed against his. Shari pulled away from his loving embrace, giggled and ran around the room so that he would chase her. The two acted as silly as the children.

—

After a couple hours of fun in the pool, Kyle and Alyssa heard the sound of their tummy's rumbling. They grabbed their towels and wrapped them around their freezing bodies. They raced each other to the elevator. Kyle won as usual. Once they were inside the elevator, they playfully pushed each other about. When they reached the fourth floor, Alyssa took off running toward their hotel room. Kyle took his sweet time. He laughed when he looked at her and waved the keycard in her face.

Time Off

"Come on, stop playing, I have to pee," she whined.

The kids entered the room and raced to the bathroom. This time Alyssa won. Soon they were both dressed and ready to feed their bellies. Wes was not eager to get out of bed. He was thoroughly relaxed and enjoying the change of scenery. He was also enjoying the football game.

"Are you coming, honey?" Shari asked him.

"I'll be down there in a sec."

"Sure," Shari said with a look of disbelief. She and the kids left the room and headed downstairs to the hotel cafeteria. The kids took off running.

"Hey, stop running," she yelled out. But the kids were too excited. They continued with their game of relay.

Soup De jour

Johnny mixed the ingredients into the soup. He stirred it with an unusual sense of enjoyment. He even hummed a happy tune.

"Boy, you must really be feeling good?" Brian commented.

Johnny smiled like someone who had just won the lottery. He continued to stir the soup and gleam with visions of quitting his dead-end job. He turned around toward the cutting board. Lost in thought, he cut down on the carrots. He did not realize how close the knife was to his finger.

"Damn it!" he shouted.

Brian rushed over to see what happened. "Here take this," Brian handed him a white cloth.

Johnny sucked the blood that poured from his cut finger. "Damn this shit stings like hell."

"I'll be right back," Brian left to find the first-aid kit.

Johnny kept his bleeding finger in his mouth. He walked over to the pot of soup that was still cooking on the stove. Worried that his delicacy would scorch, he took his finger out of his mouth to stir the vegetables and pasta around. Unknowingly, a few specks of his blood dripped into the pot.

"Here you go," Brian handed him a bottle of rubbing alcohol and a Band-Aid.

"Thanks, man."

Johnny wrapped up his bleeding finger and finished preparing the meal for the hotel patrons. He turned around and asked Brian, "Hey, tell me if I am missing anything."

Brian stepped over toward him. Johnny held the spoonful of soup up to Brian's mouth. Brian blew it and then sucked it down. "Hmm, it's pretty good." He pinched two of his fingers together and suggested, "But I would add a little more salt if I were you."

Johnny took his advice and added a pinch more salt to the pot.

—

When Shari and her children entered the hotel dining hall, she looked all around and commented, "It sure is crowded." She and the kids took a seat near the window.

The waitress soon appeared. Her smile was bright. "Hello, I'm Jennifer. I'll be your server today." She handed them all a menu. "What would you like to drink?"

"Coffee for me," Shari replied.

"Me too," Alyssa said.

Shari smiled politely and said, "She will have a glass of milk."

Kyle ordered a root beer.

"I'll be right back with your drinks. Jennifer turned around and left to gather their beverages.

"What's taking Dad so long?" Kyle asked.

"You know your father. He's probably still watching the football game."

Alyssa looked about at all the faces in the cafeteria. She smiled at the little girl seated at the table across from them. The child was friendly. She smiled at Alyssa and waved her tiny hand.

Soup De jour

"Here you go." Jennifer sat their drinks down on the table. "Are you ready to order?"

Shari looked at the menu and asked, "What is your soup of the day?"

In a slight English accent, she said, "We have delicious Borscht."

Alyssa frowned and stuck out her tongue with disgust. "What's that?"

"It is a tasty soup from Eastern Europe." The friendly waitress explained.

Both Kyle and Alyssa made faces at the thought of eating the soup.

Kindly, Shari said, "That's fine. We will just stick with the salad."

Jennifer maintained her pleasant smile, "Anything else?"

The kids ordered burgers and Shari ordered a steak with a baked potato. Jennifer reached out her hand and gathered their menus. "It shouldn't be long."

Alyssa continued to make goofy faces at the little girl across from them. Kyle talked and talked about all the new equipment he needed for his football game. Shari was thoroughly enjoying her time with the kids.

Soup De jour

Within twenty minutes of waiting, Jen-nifer reappeared with their dishes. "Enjoy," she said with a cutesy smile.

Kyle pointed toward the entrance. He was energized. "Hey, there's Dad."

"Over here," Alyssa yelled.

Wes smiled at his family and quickly joined them. As soon as he sat down, he reached over and grabbed a piece of Shari's steak off her plate.

She gently smacked his hand, "Hey, get your own," she said playfully.

Noting the new member at the table, Jennifer returned. Her smile was pleasant. "What can I get you, sir?"

Wes looked at Shari's plate. "I'll have what she is having."

"No problem. I'll be right back."

The four enjoyed their meal and chatted non-stop. Everything was perfect. They were enjoying their time away from the city. The kids quickly gobbled down their food.

Hyped, Kyle asked, "Can we go back swimming?"

Soup De jour

"You are not supposed to swim for at least an hour after eating?" Shari informed him.

"Ah, come on, Mom, we'll be fine."

"Please, Mom," Alyssa whined.

"Rules are rules," Wes stated firmly.

Disappointed, Kyle asked, "Then can we be excused?"

"And just where do you think you're going?" Shari asked.

"Since we can't go swimming, we are going to go back to the room and play video games."

"Yes, you may be excused." She warned, "But don't run."

It was too late. The kids jumped to their feet and raced all the way to the room.

Wes cut into his medium rare steak and sunk his teeth into the juicy meat. "You know there is no real medical proof that you have to wait an hour after you eat before you can swim."

"Yes, I know that, Wes, but I would rather not take any chances."

Wes looked around at all the faces in the cafeteria. He leaned over and whispered into Shari's ear, "Is it me or does some of these people look a little strange?"

Shari peered about. She let out a mild giggle and mumbled, "You're right. They look a bit ill."

Concerned, Wes said, "I hope it's not the food."

"I feel fine. What about you?" Shari asked.

"Other than my button getting ready to pop off my pants, I feel pretty damn good." Wes let out a loud burp.

"Come on, honey, show some manners."

"Lighten up, we're on vacation."

Shari shook her head. She lowered her hand under the table and rubbed the bottom of his belly.

"Stop," Wes said with a goofy grin on his face.

"Well, you said, lighten up."

They chatted for another twenty minutes. Wes wanted to hang out to allow his stomach a chance to digest. He felt stuffed and weighted from the heavy meal.

Soup De jour

Eventually, Shari turned to him. Her gaze was inviting. "Come on, let's get out of here."

"Does that mean you are going to give in and let the kids go swimming?"

Shari knew that Wes wanted to ravish her. She presented him with a wicked, little smile and batted her pretty eyes. "Give me a reason to."

He leaned over and whispered sweet nothings into her ear. She beamed from the thoughts of his seductive advances. "If you keep talking like that I will have to bribe the kids to stay in the pool all night."

They chuckled, placed their napkins next to their nearly empty plates and left the cafeteria. Wes could not help but look back. Some of the faces in the dining hall spooked him. He did not recall some of the patrons looking so pasty when he first entered the cafeteria. He did not say anything to Shari, but he was just a bit worried about the food they consumed. He hoped they would not become ill.

Once they made it back to their room, the kids, again, annoyed them about going swimming.

Soup De jour

Shari conceded, "Fine, but if you feel just the slightest cramp, get out the pool and come back to the room."

"They'll be fine," Wes added, "you worry too much."

Shari knew that he was anxious for the kids to leave. He had his own agenda. It did not take long before Alyssa and Kyle were dressed in their swimsuits and racing down the hall toward the elevators. Just as Shari predicted, Wes did not waste any time in groping and kissing her passionately.

Hounds Tooth

Kyle and his sister splashed about in the pool. They were having fun because the pool area was nearly empty. They played Marco-Polo and other fun pool games together. Before long, the pool area began to get a bit crowded. The open space they had quickly became a sardine can.

"Hey, let's go back to the room and play night stalkers?" Kyle suggested.

Agreeably, Alyssa said, "Okay."

He and Alyssa climbed out the pool. They both grabbed a towel and wrapped it around their wet, chilled bodies. They slipped on their flip-flops and left the pool area. When they entered the hall, Alyssa stopped dead in her tracks. She stared up toward the staircase.

"Hey, come on," Kyle shouted.

Alyssa did not budge.

Kyle walked back down the hall toward her. He tapped her on the shoulder. "What's wrong with you? Come on." Kyle looked over to see what had his sister's attention. When he looked over toward the stairs, he saw a man kissing on the neck of a woman. "Would you stop staring at them and come on?"

Alyssa remained frozen. Her eyes were enlarged. She looked spooked. A tear rolled down the side of her face. Kyle looked up again toward the couple on the stairs. That is when he realized why his sister was immobile with fear. When the man turned his head in their direction, his eyes were as dark as a tunnel and as large as saucers. Kyle saw blood dripping down the sides of his mouth. Kyle also noticed the lady's neck had been bitten.

On pure reflex, he snatched his sister by the hand. Frantically, he ordered, "Come on, Alyssa, run!"

They ran with all their might toward the elevators. Kyle was panicked. "Come on, Alyssa! Hurry up!" He continued to shout.

Kyle pushed and pushed the elevator button for the doors to open. In his mind, the elevator took an eternity to reach them. All the while he continued to worriedly look down the hall in hopes that the blood starved maniac was not coming their way.

Once the elevator doors opened, they quickly entered. Again, Kyle pushed the elevator button with a frightened twitch. When the doors finally closed, he turned to his sister and breathlessly asked, "What was that?"

Alyssa was unable to speak. She remained silent with fear. As soon as the button sounded off and they were on the fourth floor, they could hardly wait for the elevator door to open. Kyle and his sister ran feverishly to their hotel room.

Kyle was so terrified; he forgot he had the key-card. He banged fretfully on the door and screamed, "Let us in! Hurry up and open the door!"

Wes rushed to open the door. When he opened the door he noticed that Alyssa was nearly hyperventilating. Kyle was talking so fast, neither he nor Shari could make sense of what he was saying.

Worried, Shari ushered the kids inside and said, "Calm down. What happened?"

Wes busied himself with trying to get Alyssa to breathe normally. He rubbed her back and spoke to her calmly, "It's okay, baby, just try to relax."

Kyle looked like he had seen a ghost. He tried to explain. He pointed his finger toward the door. His chest heaved. "The man was on the stairs.....He was sucking on this lady's neck."

Wes and Shari looked at each other, assuming the man was nibbling in foreplay.

Wes calmly explained, "Son, calm down. It is not serious. Sometimes men and women kiss each other on the neck."

Kyle raised his voice, "It wasn't a kiss!" Kyle gripped his neck with his hand and screeched, "He was biting her on the neck. We saw blood!"

Alyssa was still in a state of shock. Shari walked over to her and took her into her arms. She gently rubbed her back to try to get her to relax. Alyssa looked a shade lighter and her body trembled.

Disbelieving his son, Wes suggested, "I think you guys have seen one too many scary movies. It's getting late; why don't you both lie down and get some rest?"

Kyle was adamant, "I'm telling the truth! He was sucking out her blood."

Alyssa stood stiff as a corpse. Concerned, Shari walked her to the bathroom and helped her change into her pajamas. When they rejoined Kyle and Wes, Shari pulled down the covers on the bed and told her daughter, "Come on, honey, lie down."

When Wes suggested to Kyle to try to get some rest, Kyle was reluctant to go to bed. "I'm not going to sleep. What if he comes after us?"

"Kyle, there is no one in this hotel sucking out people's blood. It is just your overactive imagination."

"I knew you wouldn't believe me. But I'm telling you, don't go out there." The look in Kyle's eyes was of pure fright.

"Go to bed, Kyle." Wes ordered.

Although Kyle climbed into bed, he refused to close his eyes. He was worried sick that the blood crazed goon would find him and drain him of his blood.

Shari continued to stroke Alyssa's hair to try to comfort her. Soon, Alyssa was deep asleep. Shari stared down at her distraught daughter. She knew that Alyssa's fear was real.

Shari walked over to Wes. Concerned, she asked, "What do you think happened?"

"Come on, Shari, they're kids. The man was probably just making out with his wife and the kids misunderstood."

"What about them seeing blood?" Shari asked.

"What do you want me to say? Some people are a little out there."

Kyle listened to his parents' conversation. He was not surprised that they doubted his story. Nevertheless, he refused to fall asleep. He continued to picture the scary image of the man in his mind. Kyle stayed awake for the next two hours, but eventually fatigue gave way. The next thing his parents' heard was his snoring.

Wes gave the matter some more thought. The more he reflected on his children's fear; he became disturbed by their strange behavior. He turned to Shari and suggested, "Maybe we should go check it out?"

"Surely, you don't believe some man was sucking blood from his wife's neck?"

"Of course not, but something sure scared the crap out the kids. It can't hurt to go take a look."

Shari shrugged and said, "What the heck, I could use a drink anyway."

Shari and Wes left their hotel room and headed toward the dining hall. Shari could not explain it, but she felt a cold shiver run up her spine. She kept turning her head from side to side. "Where is everyone?"

"It's pretty late, maybe they retired for the night," Wes said.

Shari looked all around. Her eyes were wide, "Everyone? Doesn't that seem a bit odd?"

"You're starting to sound like the kids."

Shari involuntarily sidled up closer to her husband. She continually rubbed her arms. They seemed extra cold all of a sudden. When they reached the dining hall, Shari nervously looked about. "I don't know, Wes, maybe we should head back up to the room."

"Don't tell me you are buying into all this stuff? Come on, I thought you wanted to have a drink?"

She looked at the deserted dining hall nervously and took a deep swallow. "I don't feel that thirsty anymore."

Wes fooled around. He jumped in front of her and fanned his hands wildly. In a creepy voice, he said, "I'm coming to get you, Shari."

"Please, Wes, stop. You're not funny."

"Come on, relax. There is nothing to worry about."

Wes immediately noticed the change in Shari's eyes. Her mouth hung open. She looked terrified. Then she pointed and screamed, "Wes, behind you!"

He quickly turned around. He was aghast at the appearance of the waitress that served them only a few hours ago. Her skin was pale and her eyes were sunken in and dark. Worst of all, when she opened her oversized mouth, her teeth looked like sharp ice picks. She rushed toward Wes! On pure reflex, he balled up his fist and socked her square in the jaw. She fell hard to the floor. But she did not stay down. She bounced back up to her feet like an inflatable punching bag, and charged at him again.

Shari screamed out with horror. Then before she could come to her husband's aide, she found herself fighting for her own life. Someone had approached her from behind. She could feel someone's hot breathing close upon her neck. Shari bent her arm back and punched the assailant with her elbow. She turned around to see the villain.

She could not believe her eyes. It was one of the guests she saw earlier in the cafeteria. Blood oozed down the lady's mouth. Shari was astounded by how ugly the woman looked. Just hours earlier, the woman had been beautiful and vibrant. Now she was ghastly. Her eyes were hollow and her hair stood straight up as though she stuck her finger in an electrical socket. Her mouth was so large that she could have shoved a basketball in it.

The scary looking woman grabbed a hold of Shari's arm and opened her wide mouth, exposing her razor sharp fangs. She leaned her head down to take a bite out of Shari's arm. Shari looked over and grabbed the plate from the table. She cracked the plate over the creatures' head.

"Oh my God!" Shari screamed in horror, "Wes! Wes!"

Wes had managed to beat the crap out of the vile creature that attacked him. He rushed over to Shari and helped her to fight off the fiend. He grabbed his wife by the hand. They took off running out the cafeteria as though the building was on fire.

Shari looked back; she saw the women coming after them. Fearfully, she yelled, "What is going on?"

Frantically, Wes shouted, "I don't know, but we need to get the kids and get the hell out of here."

Before they could make it to the elevator, they found themselves confronted by two more goons. Neither Shari nor Wes could believe their own eyes.

"What the hell!" Wes shouted.

Again, the two were forced to fight to the death. But no matter how many punches they threw, the darn creatures would not stay down. Wes stumped the ugly man several times in his chest. Shari kicked and shoved one of the goons over the banister into the water fountain. She rushed over and punched the elevator button.

"Come on, damn it," she cried with terror. The doors finally opened. She yelled to her husband, "Come on, Wes! Hurry up!"

Wes gave the ugly ghoul another punch and a stomp in the guts before he rushed toward the elevator. Shari pushed and pushed the button for the doors to close before one of the blood sucking freaks could enter.

Breathless and scared beyond reason, Shari cried, "This is impossible. This can't be happening."

Wes too was gasping. "We just need to get to the kids and get the hell out of here."

Both Shari and Wes could feel tightness in their chest. They were ready for anything once the door to the elevator slowly opened. Much to their horror, a blood sucker stood in front of the elevator door. Wes did not have time to think. He charged toward the ugly creature like a linebacker and pushed him over the banister. He and Shari ran toward their room. Shari's eyes were blurred due to all her tears. Wes' hand shook like a leaf on a tree. He was angered because his key-card was not working. He swiped the card again and again, but the door still would not unlock. He and Shari banged hard on the door.

Shari yelled, "Let us in! Kyle, wake up!" She constantly turned her head to look behind her in fear of what monstrous freak may be headed their way.

Wes was more verbal. He shouted, "Wake the hell up and open the damn door!"

Kyle sluggishly rolled out of bed. He walked slowly toward the door. When Shari and Wes looked back, they could see one of the ghouls headed their way.

Their knocks became intense, "Hurry, Kyle, wake up," they screamed.

Wes tried repeatedly to use the keycard but it was useless. Kyle finally opened the door. He rubbed his sleepy eyes. His parents rushed into the room. Before the door closed all the way, Kyle got a glimpse of the scary looking creature. Frightened, he peed his pants.

Wes stormed about the room like a madman in a state of shock. Scared, he shouted, "This is fucking crazy. Did you see that shit? We have to get the hell out of here!"

Shari happened to notice that Kyle was standing still in a mess of his own urine. She walked over to her son and gently touched his shoulders. She managed to calm her nerves. Her voice was docile, "Kyle, let's go to the bathroom."

Meanwhile, Wes hurried over to the telephone. His hand shook when he picked up the receiver. He yelled, "Fuck!" because all he heard was a busy signal.

Alyssa eventually awakened from the chaos. She cried out, "Mommy! Mommy!"

Shari rushed out of the bathroom. She took Alyssa into her arms and hugged her. Shari tried her hardest not to cry, but she could not help but whimper from the horrors that lurked beyond their hotel door.

Frustrated and scared, Wes kicked over a chair. He shouted with outrage, "The damn phones aren't working."

"Try the cell phone," Shari suggested.

Wes rushed over to the dresser and picked up her purse. He dumped her cluttered mess onto the dresser. Anxiously, he grabbed the cell phone and dialed 911. When he pushed the send button and listened, there was dead silence. He looked at the front of the phone with anger and yelled, "Damn it!"

Shari's eyes widened, "What's wrong?"

"I can't get any reception."

Shari looked into her daughter's scared eyes. She tried to be reassuring, "It's going to be alright." She did not want to admit that she was terrified at their fate. She walked over to Wes. Her voice was at a whisper, "We can't be the only ones still normal."

Angered and afraid, Wes snidely vented, "What do you suggest? I go out there and start knocking on people's door?" Sarcastically he said, "I'll just knock on their door and say, 'Hey, are you still human? Or would you like to take a bite out of me.'"

Shari whimpered, "I don't know what we should do!"

He quickly realized that he was taking his fears and frustrations out on his wife. He took her into his arms and apologized, "I'm sorry, baby."

"It's okay. I understand." Shari broke apart from their embrace. She solemnly walked toward the restroom to check on Kyle.

Wes was a basket case. He was clueless what to do next in order to protect his family. He timidly walked over to the window near the hotel room front door. He cautiously pulled the curtain back to peek out. What he saw was terrifying. People were running up and down the hall from ghouls. He saw the sharp fangs of one of the ugly creatures dig deep into one of the guests' neck. Horrified, he gagged and moved away from the window. He looked over at his distraught daughter. She was frozen stiff with fear. He went to her bedside and embraced her.

"It's going to be alright. Daddy won't let anything happen to you."

Shari and Kyle came from out the bathroom. Both looked petrified.

Hall of Madness

Johnny lay in bed shivering. His body felt ice cold. No matter how many blankets he placed over himself, nothing seemed to warm his chilled bones. He was desperate for Doctor Gunter to arrive. He looked over at the clock. It had been hours since he had telephoned the doctor. His condition was only getting worse. He heard a knock at his hotel door. Weak, he slowly rose up from the bed and sauntered toward the door. He pushed back the curtain to see who was knocking.

"Open up, Johnny! Let me in!"

He quickly opened the door. Liz' face displayed nothing but horror. She hurriedly entered his room and locked the door. When she turned and looked at him, she immediately became alarmed.

"What's wrong with you?" she asked with a look of fright.

He put his hand over his mouth and let out a cough, "I'm sick."

Frantic, she said, "We have to get out of here!"

Johnny staggered away and crawled back into bed. "What's wrong? You looked like you've seen a ghost."

Liz' voice was strained, "Johnny, people are eating people!"

He looked at her as if she were joking. "What are you talking about?"

Liz raced over to the nightstand and picked up the telephone. She banged the receiver down on the table in anger. "Damn it!" She looked over at Johnny. Frantic she said, "We have to get out of this hotel. I don't know what's going on but everyone is changing."

Johnny sounded tired and weak. "You're not making any sense."

She yelled and fanned her hands wildly. "They're blood suckers or something. Hell I can't explain it. All I know is that we have to get out of this hotel, now!"

"Calm down, Liz."

"Calm down?" she shouted. "You don't have a clue as to what's going on out there. I barely got away."

"Away from what?" he asked in a nonchalant tone.

"Brian, he's one of them."

Weak and not taking her serious, he asked, "Liz, you are not making any sense. Brian is one of whom?"

She screamed with fury and fear. Her eyes looked wild. She pointed toward the door. "He is one of those things out there!"

Suddenly there was a banging noise at the door. Liz nearly jumped out of her skin. Her eyes looked crazed. She put her finger on her lip gesturing for Johnny to remain silent. She whispered, "Don't answer it."

"Get a grip, Liz."

Johnny slowly crawled out of bed and strolled toward the door. Liz walked so close to his back, she stepped on the heel of his foot.

"Calm down, Liz."

Liz begged, in a low tone, "Please, Johnny, whatever you do, don't open the door."

Noting her genuine fear, he crept toward the window. He peeked out through the crack of the curtain and thought for sure that he was having a bad head trip. He could not believe the horrible sight of his buddy.

Brian placed his bloody hand on the glass. He looked ghastly. Blood was all around his mouth. His clothes were torn and bloody as well. Johnny leaped back from the curtain. His heart skipped a beat. He appeared to turn a shade lighter.

Liz was still close upon him. Whispering and pointing hysterically, she said, "You see. I told you. People are out there eating each other!"

Frightened, Johnny asked, "What the heck is going on?"

"I don't know. But I'm scared, Johnny. What are we going to do?"

Johnny rushed over to the telephone. Full of rage and fear, he snatched the telephone off the nightstand and threw it against the wall because it still had a busy signal. He began to pace nervously around the room.

"Okay, let's not panic. I called Doctor Gunter. He should be here soon." Hopeful, he said, "Once he sees all the chaos, he will call the police."

Liz looked baffled, "Who is Doctor Gunter?"

Johnny recalled Doctor Gunter telling him not to mention the experiment to anyone. But at this point, it did not seem to matter much if he revealed the Doctor's secret. Johnny divulged everything to Liz about his involvement with the doctor.

Liz was shocked. "You mean to tell me that you allowed yourself to be a Guinea pig?"

"I needed the extra cash. I didn't see any harm in it."

"You don't think that somehow that has something to do with what is going on here do you?"

Perplexed, Johnny said, "How could it?" He began to think hard. He paced back and forth in the tiny room. All of a sudden, it was as if a light turned on in his head. He looked down at his wrapped finger and muttered, "Oh shit!"

"What? What is it?" Liz asked desperate for answers.

Johnny turned around to face her. He looked devastated. "It's me!"

"What do you mean?" Liz asked her face a mask of confusion.

Johnny held up his wounded finger. His tone was high pitched, "I cut my finger when I was preparing the food." He looked grave as he recalled, "I was stirring the soup. My blood must have gotten into it."

"I don't understand, Johnny, why would that have anything to do with what is going on out there?"

Embittered and equally desperate to make sense of the madness unfolding, he remarked, "What if the injections Doctor

89

Gunter gave me somehow caused this? Think about it. My blood spilled into the food. Now people are raving lunatics. It must have something to do with the injections he gave me."

Johnny could instantly see the fear emerging in Liz's eyes. She began to step away from him.

Suddenly, he gripped the bottom of his stomach and bowled over. There was a terrible cramp causing him immense pain. He cried out in agony, "Oh God, what's happening to me?"

Liz continued to stare at him with great trepidation. Her eyes roamed around the room. She was flustered. She knew it was not safe to go back out into the hall, but it appeared she was no safer in the room with Johnny.

He reached out his hand to her and cried out, "Help me."

She continued to step back away from him. Her eyes grew as large as owl's. She warned, "Keep away from me, Johnny. I don't want to hurt you but I will."

Johnny begged, "Liz, please, I need your help."

She balled her fist and raised her hands, "Stay back!" she warned.

Johnny was weak and hunched over in pain. He begged, "Please, Liz. I'm not one of them. I just need help."

There was a part of her that felt empathy for him. Although she was scared of what he may transform into, she wanted to help him. Hesitantly, she put down her guard and stepped closer to him. She then took a hold of his arm and helped him over to the bed.

Realizing how weak he was, she no longer feared him. She put a blanket over his shivering body. She hurried to the bathroom and poured him a glass of water. When she returned to his bedside and handed him the water, he could barely hold the glass. She helped to hold the glass up to his lips.

Distressed, she said, "Johnny, I don't think the doctor is coming."

Johnny sadly admitted, "Neither do I."

Liz was shaking with fear. "This is so screwed up. We have to get out of here."

She crept over toward the window. When she looked out into the hall, she could see a few people running about. She knew from the terrorized look upon their faces that they were running for their lives.

—

Wes and Shari jumped out of their skin from the screams at their hotel door. The distress and fear was evident in the voices from the other side of the door.

Wes looked over at Shari and his children. He ordered her, "Take them to the back."

"You're not going to let them in are you?" Shari asked fretfully.

He raised his voice, "Just get the kids to the back."

The voices on the other side of their hotel door were urgent. The scared group banged on the door and begged, "Please, let us in, they're coming!"

Wes peeked out through the curtain. He saw four terror struck faces. But the sight of the young girl hurt him the most. The panic in their voices was heart-wrenching. When Wes looked harder, he could see a few blood suckers fast approaching the frightened group. If he was going to allow them entrance he had to do it now or never. Wes quickly opened the door and let the scared people inside. He hurriedly locked the door behind them. The group stood panting hard. Wes stood back from them in a defensive position. He was ready to beat the hell out of them if they made one false move.

Hunched over, sweaty and breathless, the young man said, "Thanks, man. I don't know what the hell is going on."

The females looked terrified. They sobbed uncontrollably.

"Who are you"? Wes asked.

Still gasping, the young man said, "My name is Maxwell." He turned and pointed, "This is my girlfriend, Ashley, my sister, Kelli and her daughter, Amber. We just checked in today." Maxwell wheezed. His voice was full of suffering, fear, confusion and disbelief. "I just wanted to do something nice for my girl."

He stared at Wes with crazed eyes. "How could it turn into something like this?"

The women listlessly walked over to the sofa. They slumped down on the small coach. Kelli rocked back and forth, hugging her daughter tightly. She sobbed hysterically. The flashbacks of her husband being eaten alive were too much to bear.

Maxwell looked horrified. Seeking answers, he asked, "What the heck are those things?"

At first Wes did not respond. He continued to stare at him inquisitively.

Worried, Maxwell insisted, "Hey, I'm not one of those things." Maxwell looked deranged. His voice was loud, "One of those freaking things ate my sister's husband!"

"Sorry, dude, but this is some strange shit."

Maxwell agreed. "Tell me about it."

Eventually, Shari came from out the back room. She noticed the two frantic looking women and the young girl sitting on the sofa. All of them looked so frightened. Shari caringly walked over to them.

Ashley looked up at Shari and then she looked at Kelli. She somberly explained to Shari, "They ate her husband."

Shari sat down beside Kelli. When the rattled woman looked into Shari's sympathetic eyes her cries intensified.

Wes and Maxwell walked away from the women toward the bathroom.

"Any ideas on how we get out of this mess?" Maxwell asked.

Wes looked stumped, "I'm open to suggestions."

Kyle and Alyssa opened the door of the back bedroom. Wes lovingly looked at his children. He fanned his hand for them to come out. He introduced the young man to his children. "Max, this is my son, Kyle, and my daughter, Alyssa."

Maxwell nodded his head toward them. The kids went to the open area and sat beside their mother. Alyssa seemed to gravitate to the young girl. She quickly sat by her side. Caringly, Alyssa patted Amber's hand.

Maxwell felt terrible. It was bad enough that adults were trapped in this nightmare, but he hated that kids were caught up in this madness as well.

Blood Lust

Carl yelled at his wife. "Katherine, what in the hell is all that damn racket about?"

Katherine stepped out from the bathroom. She spoke loudly over the sound of her blow-dryer. "I don't know."

"Well, damn it, find out. Don't you see I'm trying to rest?" Sounding every bit the grouch, he demanded, "Call down to the front desk and make a complaint. I'm not spending my money to hear all that damn ruckus."

Katherine let out a sigh of annoyance. She turned off the blow-dryer and slowly walked over to the credenza. She picked up the telephone. "Hmm," she muttered.

Carl shouted, "What did they say?"

She yelled back to him, "I got a busy signal. I'll try to call back in a few minutes."

"Do I have to do everything myself?" He grunted. He angrily rolled out of bed, slipped on his expensive slippers and walked to the front door of their hotel room. "Damn kids," he snarled.

He opened the door with every intention of going down to the main lobby to complain about the unruly guest. However, as soon as he opened the door, he saw nothing but madness in the hall. He stuttered with complete disbelief, "What the hell!" He instantly closed the door shut and double locked it. When he turned around, Katherine stood before him with her blow-dryer in hand.

She stared into his deranged eyes. "What's the matter, honey?"

For a split second he was speechless. The words were caught in his throat. His body was unmoving. Katherine walked toward him. When she reached out her hand for the door knob, he slapped her hand away and grumbled, "No, don't!"

Stunned by his odd behavior, she asked, "What has gotten in to you?"

She shoved him aside and peered out the glass window. There was no way she could conceive what her eyes were witnessing. She blinked in the hopes that she was seeing incorrectly. Her mouth instantly went dry. She stumbled backward away from the window.

Carl continued to stand and shake like paper in the wind.

"Oh, my God, What are they doing?" she squealed.

Carl ran over to the telephone. He picked it up and pushed zero for the operator. "Damn it!" He roared with anger. He slammed the receiver down.

Katherine could not help herself; she looked through the small crack from the curtain again. She was horrified at what she saw.

"Get away from there!" Carl shouted.

"What is that? What are they doing?" Her heart began to thump hard against her chest. "Oh God, Carl, we have to get out of here."

"Where's your cell phone?" he asked anxiously.

She squealed, "You told me not to bring it."

Peeved, he yelled, "Since when in the hell did you start listening to me?"

He took baby steps toward the window. Although he was reluctant to witness the lunacy unfolding, he could not help but take another peek. Once he did look through the cracked curtain; he gasped in awe. One of the ugly creatures had his face up against the glass window. Once the vile creature saw Carl, he stuck out his long bloody tongue and licked the glass hungrily.

Carl jumped back with fright. "Oh shit!"

Katherine was horrified. She looked like a frightened little girl. Her tone of voice sounded like a whinny child, "Carl....., what are we going to do? We can't stay here."

Scared, he yelled, "Don't you think I know that?"

Katherine headed back toward the window. Carl immediately strong armed her and stopped her. "Stay away from that damn window!" He walked over to the mini-bar and downed two tiny bottles of scotch.

"This is no time to be drinking," she shrieked.

"Trust me, Katherine; this is the perfect time for a drink."

He held out a small bottle of booze to her. She slothfully walked over to him and took the tiny bottle from his hand. She had no trouble downing the miniature bottle of gin.

Still in a state of disbelief, Carl muttered, "This can't be happening."

Equally stunned, Katherine asked, "What are they, Carl?"

"The hell if I know. But whatever they are, we don't want any parts of them."

Carl walked to the back room and stepped out onto the balcony. He looked downward. He knew there was no way they could jump without being hurt or worse. Katherine stood stiffly in the center of the front room. It felt as though the room was spinning. Eyes bulged, she looked confused and terrified. Quickly, she struggled to push the sofa in front of the door.

Carl rushed toward her, grabbed her by the arm and turned her around to face him. His voice was shaky and low, "What are you doing?"

She looked insane. "I'm not going to make it easy for them to eat me."

Snidely, he remarked, all while keeping his voice at a whisper, "If they really want to get in, I'm sure the window would be a preferable choice."

Katherine was losing it. Her eyes were full of fear. She cried, "What are we going to do? Tell me, Carl, how in the hell are we going to get out of this mess?"

Frustrated and scared, he grunted, "Calm down and let me think, damn it."

Escape Plan

Maxwell evaluated the distance from the balcony to the ground. "Okay, there is no way we can jump from this height."

Wes looked down with disappointment. "I know, but we damn sure can't stay locked up in this room. The phones aren't working and who knows if or when help will arrive."

Maxwell rushed toward the beds. He began taking off all the blankets and sheets. Wes followed his lead. The men frantically

began tying the sheets and blankets together.
Soon, they had what equated to a long rope.

"What if we get climb down and there are more of those things?" Wes commented.

Maxwell's eyes were solemn. "I don't see that we have much of a choice."

"I hear you, man. Where is your car?" Wes asked.

Maxwell and Wes walked over to the balcony. Maxwell pointed, "From here, it is just across the lot. It's the red SUV. But there is only one problem."

Escape Plan

Wes looked straight into his eyes fretfully.

Maxwell could tell from the look Wes displayed just what he was thinking. "Yep, the keys are back in my room," Maxwell said.

"Fuck!" Wes shouted. "We need those keys. Our car is too far away. We can't risk it."

"I don't know. Going out there is just as risky."

Wes walked toward the front room window. He looked into the hall. He saw a few of the blood suckers roaming about. He walked back to the room where he found Maxwell looking perturbed. Wes walked upon him and whispered, "What floor are you on?

"We're just around the bend."

"I bet we can get to your room. We're both strong and if we arm ourselves, we can get past those few blood suckers. We have to try. It's only a matter of time before they find a way in."

"This is some really fucked up shit," Maxwell declared.

Wes looked desperate. "I have to get my family out of here. Are you with me or not?"

Escape Plan

Maxwell looked over at the children. He looked into Ashley and Kelli's frantic eyes. He turned to Wes confidently and replied, "Yeah, man, I'm with you."

Wes knew convincing Shari of his plan would not be easy. He walked over to her with his head held slightly downward, "Hey, I need to speak with you."

Shari slowly stood up. She gave Kelli a supportive tap on the shoulder. The children remained seated. Alyssa continued to sit next to Amber. Wes and Shari walked to the back room where Maxwell paced about nervously.

Wes began to slowly explain his plan to Shari. "Baby, Max and I were talking."

Shari immediately looked alarmed.

Wes stared deeply into her sad brown eyes. "Babe, listen to me. We can't just sit here. It is only a matter of time before those things start pounding on the window and break in."

Her voice trembled with fear. "What are you suggesting?"

Wes took her by the hand and walked her over to the balcony. He pointed. "See that red car across the lot?"

"Yes, I see it."

"That's Maxwell's car. We can all get in it and drive away from this place."

Shari knew there was more.

Wes took her by the arms and turned her around to face him. He stared deep into her eyes. "Look, we have to get to Maxwell's car." He pointed at the tied sheets and blankets. "All we need to do is climb down and run like hell."

Slightly hopeful, she asked, "Do you think we can make it?"

"We have too."

121

Maxwell turned his head because he knew that Wes was a bit worried about telling her the rest of their plan.

Wes kissed Shari's lips and continued to look intensely into her scared brown eyes. "Babe, there is just one problem." He paused slightly before saying, "Max's keys are in his room."

"What!"

"Shih, calm down and listen to me. His room is just on the other side of the hall. We can make it."

Escape Plan

Shari could not help but raise her voice, "Have you completely lost your mind? We barely made it out of the cafeteria. From what I can see, their numbers have doubled."

"Shari, we don't have any other options."

Her eyes were filled with fear and tears. She looked over at Maxwell. He remained silent. She stared deeply into her husband's eyes. "Are you sure this is the only way?"

"Yes. I'm sure," Wes said.

Although she was scared beyond reason, she understood that her husband was correct. They were sitting ducks. She believed, just as Wes, that it was only a matter of time before the blood sucking freaks teamed up and finished off the remaining survivors. She turned around and grabbed an object off the dresser. Wes and Maxwell looked perplexed.

"Here," she handed Wes a can of hair-spray.

Both men looked at her as if she were nuts.

Wes looked stupefied. "What am I supposed to do with this?" he asked clearly confused.

Escape Plan

"Spray them in the eyes. They won't be able to see."

Wes smiled and kissed her for her effort. "Thanks, babe," he looked around the room. "What else do we have?"

The only thing they could find was the iron. Maxwell grabbed it. He sucked in a deep breath. He looked like a frightened cat. "I guess this is it." Maxwell left the back room and went to speak with Ashley and Kelli. Once he approached his sister; Kyle and Alyssa walked away to join their parents.

Maxwell kneeled down before his distraught sister. She was still crying uncontrollably. He reached out his hand and gently touched the side of her frightened face. Lovingly, he said, "Hey, Wes and I are going to go to the room and get the keys to the car."

Ashley instantly objected, "There is no way you are going out there."

Maxwell turned his head and looked over at her. His voice was stern, "Listen to me. We can't just sit here and wait to be eaten."

"Don't go out there, Uncle Max," Amber somberly said.

Escape Plan

He looked at his niece with nothing but love. He gently stroked the side of her innocent face. "I promise I won't let them get me. I will be back for you and your mommy."

Amber's heart felt heavy with fear. She had just lost her father and now she may lose her uncle as well. Tears rolled down her sad face.

Kelli was so grief stricken; she could only sob even harder. Terrible images of her husband being eaten alive obsessed her. She looked into her brother's eyes. She begged, "Don't leave me, Max."

Maxwell was in a terrible spot. He did not want to leave the women, but he knew he needed to make a move to try to save them. He tenderly caressed his sister's distressed face. "I promise, Kelli, I will be back to get you out of here." He stood up and walked over to Ashley.

Ashley's eyes were flooded with worry and tears. She begged, "Please be careful."

He kissed her quivering lips and vowed, "I won't leave here without you. We are all going to get out of this nightmare."

She embraced him tightly and whispered in his ear, "I love you."

He looked deeply into her panicky eyes. His voice was soft, "I love you too." He hated to see how worried she was. He held up her chin. His smile was bright. Jokingly he said, "I'll be back before you can say *Momma needs a new pair of shoes.*"

He was just a bit relived to see her grin at his silly comment. He then gave her a passionate tongue kiss. He kissed her as if it were their last kiss. Although Ashley did not say another word, she feared she would never see him again.

In the Closet

Nora continued to peek through the keyhole of the broom closet. She saw one of the ugly blood suckers lurking about. She turned to Bobby, "It's only one of them now. I bet we could take him."

"Are you crazy? You saw what they did to Marie. I'm not about to get ate by one of those things."

Nora was pissed at his cowardly behavior. "Then what do you plan to do? We can't stay here."

"Why not? They haven't found us so far," he replied.

"Look, Bobby, these things are all over the place. It's only a matter of time before they burst through this door. I have no desires to be eaten and turn into one of those ugly fucking creatures."

"So what do you suggest? We go out there and try to fight our way through?"

Firmly, she said, "Yes that is exactly what I think."

"I don't happen to agree with you. If you want to run out there and get ripped apart, be my guest, but I think I'll take my chances right here."

Nora stormed upon him. She was livid. "You had better grow some balls you spineless little shit. Now I'm telling you there is only one of those things out there. We can take him and get to a phone to call for help."

At this point, Bobby was more afraid of Nora than the ugly ghoul outside the door. He put his hands in the air in a surrendering fashion, "Fine, okay, just calm down."

Nora's eyes frantically darted around the small space. She ordered, "Find something to fight with."

Smart mouthed, Bobby picked up a broom, "Hey, I can always sweep him to death."

Nora was in no mood for jokes. She snatched the broom from his hand and broke it over her knee. There was a sharp point on the broken ends. She handed one half to Bobby. She looked serious and ready to fight. "Are you ready?"

In the Closet

He was impressed with her wittiness. He shook with fear. "No, but I suppose we had better get it over with."

"Okay, on the count of three. One, two, three," she quickly opened the closet door!

The deformed looking man leaped to-ward them with his large, sharp teeth exposed and his eyes blood-shot red with rage.

Bobby yelled like a little girl, "Oh shit; oh shit."

Nora was treacherous. She kicked and jabbed the crazed man in the stomach. Once the creature fell to the floor, Bobby stomped him several times and stuck his broom stick through his heart. Blood shot up in Bobby's face. Bobby squealed and frantically wiped the blood away from his eyes. "You freak!"

The duo took off running. They made it as far at the stairs before they were confronted by two more blood suckers.

Bobby yelled at Nora, "I told you we should have stayed in the closet!"

Nora had no time to argue with him. She fought off one of the blood suckers. Bobby was left to fend for himself. His fear must have provided him with strength because when the blood sucking freak came his way, he punched him so hard, the creature fell to the floor. Bobby didn't stop there. He stomped the creature in the head with his big foot and heavy steel-toed boot over and over again. He continued to scream, "You sick freak!"

Nora and Bobby ran through the first door they came upon. They ran up the stairs. When they made it to the fourth floor; Nora opened the door very slowly.

Bobby stood close to her backside breathing hard. He whispered, "What do you see?"

Keeping her voice equally low, she said, "Nothing, it looks safe."

They cautiously entered the hall. But within seconds of having stepped out into the hallway, all hell broke loose.

Bobby looked at the creepy monsters running toward them, and screamed, "Run Nora, Run!"

From all accounts it looked like he and Nora were outnumbered. As tough as Nora was, this was one battle he was sure the blood suckers would win. He and Nora fought vigorously for their lives.

Nora screamed with each punch she threw, "You sick bastards. I won't die this way."

Wes and Maxwell heard the commotion. They looked out the window. They could see that the couple just a few feet outside their door was in need of help.

Wes turned to Maxwell. His chest heaved. "Are you ready?"

"As ready as I'll ever be," Maxwell muttered.

Wes looked over at the lamp that sat on the table. Although he truly appreciated his wife's efforts, he felt like a wimp carrying a bottle of hairspray for his defense. He quickly put down the bottle of spray and grabbed the iron lamp. Maxwell opened the door and the men headed full throttle to help the couple fight off the goons.

Shari and Ashley looked out the window with wide eyes and pure terror constricting their chests. Kelli was immobile. She sat on the sofa full of dread that she would lose her brother to the blood sucking freaks.

Although Maxwell could not hear her, Ashley screamed frightfully, "Watch out, Max!"

Kyle rose from the sofa. Shari instantly turned around, grabbed him by the arm and led him and Alyssa to the back room. She did not want them to witness the brutality and madness that was unfolding outside their door. Ashley banged on the glass because one of the ghouls was about to take a bite out of Maxwell's arm. A few of the goons turned to look at her, and then they rushed toward the window like a wild pack of wolves. Wes, Maxwell, Nora and Bobby fought off the remaining blood suckers.

Maxwell broke through the crowd and made it to his hotel room. He frantically dug in his pocket for his keycard. Once he had the door to his room opened, he yelled to the group, "Come on, and hurry up!"

The three kicked and shoved their way to reach Maxwell's room. Once they entered, all were breathless and sweaty from the battle.

In the Closet

Bobby fell down to the floor. He leaned his back against the door and let out a huge sigh, "Thank God!"

Nora looked at both Wes and Maxwell. Full of gratitude, she said, "Thank you. I don't know what we would have done if you hadn't shown up."

Bobby would not let up. He looked at Nora and vented, "I told you, we should have just stayed in the closet."

Annoyed and physically drained, Nora turned to him and shouted, "Would you shut the hell up about that damn closet!"

"Hey, everyone is scared," Maxwell commented in his effort to try to ease the tension. He then looked over at the nightstand, grabbed his car keys and quickly put them in his pants pocket.

"Now what?" Bobby asked.

Wes was firm, "Now we get the hell out of here."

Nora's tone was full of desperation. "What do you have in mind?"

Wes explained, "Maxwell has a car right outside my hotel room. We are going to climb down from the balcony, get to his car and get the hell out of here."

Worried about himself, Bobby asked, "Is there enough room for all of us?"

Nora was disgusted with his apparent selfishness. "You know what, Bobby, I have a good mind to open this door and throw your ass out to those things."

"Hey, don't go picking on me," he whined.

"Everybody, just calm down," Wes yelled.

Maxwell set Bobby's mind at ease. "Yes, there is enough room for all of us."

Bobby released a large breath of relief.

—

Katherine walked out onto the balcony. She yelled, "Hello, can anybody hear me?" She repeated, "Hello, please somebody, we need help."

"Shih," Maxwell remarked, "Do you hear that?"

Wes and Maxwell swiftly walked to the back room toward the balcony. Wes slid open the balcony doors. When he and Maxwell looked about, they saw an attractive woman leaning over the balcony railing just above them.

"Are you alright"? Maxwell yelled back.

"Oh, thank God," she said with relief. "Yes, we're okay."

Wes yelled, "How many of you are there?"

She shouted over the banister, "Just me and my husband."

Maxwell whispered, "Hey man, we can't take anyone else. There isn't enough room."

Nora and Bobby joined the men. Nora feared for the couple above them. She looked at Maxwell. "What are we going to do?"

"We will just have to send back help," Maxwell told her.

Bobby was the ultimate pessimist. "Do you have any idea how far away we are from civilization? By the time we reach help and send them back, they'll all be blood curdling creatures."

Nora turned to face him. Her face was venomous. "If you don't shut up already!"

Maxwell yelled up at the woman, "Do you have a cell phone?"

"No, I didn't bring one."

"Damn it!" Maxwell muttered.

"It wouldn't do any good. Nothing is working out here," Wes informed him.

Carl walked over to Katherine. "Who are you talking to?"

Optimistic, she said, "There are some people just below us."

"Do they have any idea how we can get out of this mess?"

Her tone was edgy. "I don't know, Carl."

Carl shoved her aside. He leaned over the banister and gruffly said, "Hey down there. My name is Carl Witherspoon. I will give each of you ten thousand dollars if you can get me and my wife out of here safely."

In the Closet

Wes was just a bit peeved by his rich man's attitude. He shouted back, "We all want to get out of here."

Nora was equally annoyed. She muttered, "God, what a pompous ass."

"What we need to do is get back to the ladies and the kids," Maxwell stated.

Bobby walked back to the front room and peeked out the side of the curtain.

Close behind him, Nora whispered, "What do you see?"

Smart mouthed, "What do you think I see? Blood sucking freaks waiting for us to come out so they can eat us for dinner."

Disheartened, the duo walked to the back room and rejoined Maxwell and Wes.

Wes was insistent. "I have to get back to my wife and kids."

"Yeah, and I can't leave Ashley and my sister," Maxwell added.

Again, Bobby smart-mouthed, "Well unless you have wings and can fly, I don't think you will be going anywhere any time soon."

In the Closet

Tempers were high. Maxwell had found Bobby's smart mouth attitude a bit disturbing. Maxwell angrily walked upon him. His eyes were dilated and his nostrils flared, "If you don't shut the hell up, we will use you as their next meal."

Bobby stepped back from his mean face. He fanned his hands in the air, "Okay, okay, calm down."

"Are you still there?" Carl shouted.

Wes hollered back up to him, "We're still here."

Gruffly, Carl asked, "So do we have a deal?"

"Look, your money is no good to anyone right about now. If we get out, we will send back help."

Carl roared, "We'll be dead by the time you find help."

Wes said nothing further.

Fiend at My Door

Liz hoped Johnny would get better and soon. Otherwise, he was going to prove completely useless against whatever fate awaited them. She helped him to lie back down on the bed. The more time passed, the sicker he became. His skin was pasty. There were dark circles under his blood-shot eyes. He looked frail and weak. Reluctant, she walked back over to the window and peeked out the small crack of the curtain. She was relieved that Brian was gone.

She considered making a run for it. Then she looked back over at Johnny's sickly body. Her heart sank. She wanted to help him but she was beginning to feel he was more of a burden.

She walked over to him. His eyes were half shut. She shook him lightly on the shoulder. "Johnny, Johnny, can you hear me?"

His voice was weak. "Yeah, I can hear you."

"Johnny, I need to try to get help."

Panicked, Johnny protested, "No, don't go out there."

Liz was adamant, "I have to. We can't stay cooped up in here."

Feebly, he begged, "Please, don't leave me."

Liz was guilt ridden. She did not want to leave him, but she knew if he were to go with her it would only be a death sentence. Johnny was in no shape to defend himself.

Angered, she yelled, "Crap! Where is that damn doctor?"

Johnny looked pitiful. "Forget about him. He is not coming."

"How could he have done something so despicable?"

She turned away from Johnny and walked to the back room. She opened the balcony door and looked about. All seemed lifeless. She looked straight down from the balcony. She knew she could not jump from that height. Dismayed, she walked back into the room where Johnny lay shivering.

She continued to vent her frustrations. "Why did this place have to be out in the middle of nowhere?"

Fiend at My Door

Johnny was on the verge of uncon-sciousness. He no longer responded to her ranting. Liz knew she was on her own. She walked back over to the thick glass plated window. At a snail's pace, she pulled back the corner of the curtain. She did not see a soul in sight. She took a look back over at Johnny. She had no desire to just sit around and wait for help. Determined, one way or another she was going to get out of the hotel from hell. Her eyes roamed all about the room in search of a weapon. She saw Johnny's sports bag lying on the floor in the corner. She raced over to it. Relieved, she pulled out his metal baseball bat. She swung it about in the air several times, "That's right; take this, you zombie freaks."

—

Carl's ego took a hit when the people below him did not succumb to his bribe. He was use to buying whatever he wanted and that included the cooperation of others. He angrily turned around and stomped back into the room like a petulant child.

"Now what?" Katherine asked irritably.

Equally pestiferous, he barked, "How in the hell should I know."

Both Carl and Katherine nearly jumped out of their skin. There was a loud bang on the front room glass window.

Carl placed his finger on his lips, "Shih."

Katherine looked completely petrified. Her eyes were bulged and her chest rose up and down from fear. Carl crept over toward the window. He cautiously pulled back the curtain just a pinch. He leaped back and held his chest! He turned whiter than a sheet of paper.

Frantic from his reaction, Katherine fearfully muttered, "What is it?"

Carl did not utter a word. He instantly ran to the back room. His hands shook uncontrollably. He ripped off the sheets from the beds.

Katherine could not help herself. She walked over toward the window. Her stomach was full of jitters. Very slowly, she pulled back the curtain. The site was absolutely horrifying. She put her hands up to her mouth and let out the most horrendous scream, "Oh, my God!"

Fiend at My Door

One of the creepy bloodsuckers was banging someone's decapitated head against the glass. Katherine rushed to the back room. She frantically began helping Carl tie the bed sheets together.

Carl's panic kicked into high gear. "Hurry, damn it, Hurry!"

Their hands trembled with unadulterated fear as they hastily tied the sheets in knots.

Carl rushed over to the balcony. He yelled with fright, "Are you there? Are you still there?"

Wes and the others could hear the terror and utter fear in his voice. They raced to the back room.

"What's going on?" Wes shouted.

"We're coming down."

"Wait a minute," Maxwell yelled.

"There's no time. We have to get out of here!"

"What's going on up there?" Wes asked.

Carl's voice was shaky. "They're banging on the glass."

"Oh shit," Nora muttered.

The banging intensified and got increasingly louder. Carl yelled at his wife, "Get over here." He fanned his hand motioning for her to put a move on it, "Hurry up!"

Katherine ran over to the balcony and they quickly tied the sheets to the railing.

"Come on, hurry it up," he said fretfully. He took her hand and helped her over the banister.

She clung desperately to the sheets for dear life. She dangled about, kicking her skinny legs wildly. Maxwell and Wes stood on the balcony below waiting for her body to lower so they could grab hold of her. Just as they took hold of her frail, quivering body, there was a loud crashing sound.

"What was that?" Wes yelled up at Carl.

Suddenly, all they could hear were Carl's screams of agony as he was mercilessly torn apart by the hungry beast. Wes and Maxwell frantically helped Katherine to safety. Just when they helped her down from the makeshift rope, one of the bloodsuckers looked over the balcony down at them. The ugly creature hissed with pleasure and licked his bloody lips. Drips of blood oozed out of the sides of his mouth.

"Oh fuck!" Wes and Maxwell shouted in chorus.

Katherine did not waste any time. She quickly ran inside the room. Maxwell was close behind her. Wes hastily closed and locked the balcony doors.

"We have to go. They're coming!" Maxwell shouted frightfully.

Once again Bobby spurted out with a childlike whine, "I knew I should have stayed in the closet."

167

The bloodsuckers crawled down the knotted sheets onto the balcony. They banged viciously on the glass door. The glass was not as thick as the plated glass in the front. After a few more of the bloodsuckers joined in, their combined force began to shatter the glass. Wes and the others knew they had no choice but to make a run for it.

Wes opened the front door and within seconds the group was in the hall and confronted by blood crazed ghouls. Maxwell and the others punched, kicked, slapped and fought to the death.

Fiend at My Door

—

Liz decided that she had no choice. She gripped the bat tightly in her hand. She sucked in a large breath. Her hand shook as she slowly unlocked the door and turned the knob. Cautiously, she opened the door. Her eyes bopped all around the hall searching for the evil creatures. She quietly stepped into the hall. All was silent. She ran with all the fear of a thief in the night. She reached the emergency exit. Hurriedly, she opened the door and ran down the staircase. Suddenly, she came to a screeching halt. A couple of the blood crazed zombies were coming up the stairwell. When they caught site of her, they grinned fiendishly and increased their speed.

Liz retreated and ran back up the stairs. Scared beyond reason, she quickly opened the door to the fourth floor. Much to her shock there was a massive battle in action. There was no time to turn around and run. She quickly decided to join forces with the battling crew. She swung her bat and went ape on the bloodsuckers behind her. Then she entered the hall and beat the crap out of one of the monsters that came lunging toward her.

Wes and Maxwell gave a few of the creatures some serious head blows and strong punches in the face. The fight was fierce as the battle moved down the hall. Shari and Ashley looked out the window in complete horror. Eventually Kelli got up off the sofa to see what was happening. When she caught a glimpse of the madness in the hall, she feared she would lose her brother to the vile creatures of the night. The women watched Maxwell sock one of the ghouls in the face. Then another demon jumped on Maxwell's back. He turned violently to try to get the hellion off him. Soon, he was out numbered.

Kelli screamed out with horror and fear for her brother's life. Without forethought, she grabbed the can of hairspray off the table.

Shari pleaded, "Don't go out there!"

Kelli's tears intensified. She ignored Shari's plea. She opened the door and rushed out into the hall amidst the madness. She ran straight toward Maxwell. He twirled around madly to try to get the fiend off his back. Kelli beat the hellion with her fist. When the creature turned his head, she sprayed its eyes with the hair spray. The ghoul let out a screeching cry. It let go of Maxwell and grabbed its burning eyes. Kelli then kicked the freak several times in the gut. Eventually the demon fell to the floor. She and Maxwell stomped and beat it merciless. The crew fought ferociously all while making their way toward Wes' room.

Heart pounding hard against his chest, Wes yelled at the group, "Come on!"

Katherine was the first to follow Wes' lead. She noticed the ladies staring out the window of the room. Katherine hauled ass toward safety. Eventually, the others fought their way through the ghouls. Shari hurriedly opened the door. All were breathless as they ran for dear life.

Once the door was shut and all were safely inside, Bobby leaned his back against the door, sweating profusely, breathlessly, he asked, "Now what? We can't all fit into the car."

Everyone's head seemed to turn and focus on him.

He raised his hand in the air. "Hey, I am just saying."

Fiend at My Door

"Shut up, Bobby," Nora yelled full of annoyance.

Maxwell quickly embraced his sister. "You know you shouldn't have left the room."

She sobbed, "I wasn't going to let you be eaten by one of those freaks."

He continued to hug her.

Ashley slothfully walked over to them. She put her arms around them both.

Loud bangs hammered the window. Wes yelled to Shari, "Get the kids! We have to go now!"

Maxwell and Nora rushed to the back room. With the speed of lightening, they tied the makeshift rope around the balcony railing.

"Hurry!" Maxwell hollered fearfully. "Come on, we have to go!"

The bangs became more intense.

"Oh, shit!" Bobby stammered. He scooted up off the floor. He rose to his feet very slowly. His body quivered with each step he took toward the window. When he pushed the curtain back just a bit, he saw one of the demons beating the window with Liz's steel bat. "Shit!"

Fiend at My Door

Wes shouted out orders to the women. He instructed, "Maxwell and I will climb down first and make sure the coast is clear."

The group moved fast. Maxwell and Wes had no trouble climbing down the make-shift rope. Once they landed on the ground, they became quiet as mice. Eyes wide, hearts pounding hard, sweat pouring; they looked about the vast darkness fearfully. Their eyes darted about frantically in the hopes that none of the starved crazed goons were near-by. They did not hear or see anything strange.

Shari lowered Kyle over the banister. He climbed down like a pro. But things changed dramatically when it was time to lower Alyssa.

Alyssa whined, "I can't, Mommy."

Shari's mouth was dry and her heart felt as though it would pop out of her chest. She knew there was no time to waste. She pleaded, "Please, Alyssa, you can do it. Now hurry, baby."

"No, Mommy, I'll fall."

"No you won't, baby."

The sounds of the thumps against the window intensified. There was little doubt that the glass would soon give way to the brut force.

Bobby knew they had no time to spare. The glass was starting to crack. He sprang into action. He managed to keep his voice steady. He even conjured up a warm smile. He looked at Alyssa caringly, "What if I let you ride on my back?"

Alyssa looked so timid and scared.

Bobby reassured her, "I promise if you hold on tightly around my neck, I won't let you fall."

There was another loud bang against the window. Time was of the essence.

Shari pleaded, "Please, Alyssa, we have to go!"

Bobby could not continue to waste time. He bent down before Alyssa, maintaining his kind grin. He used his hand to make a cross sign across his chest. "I cross my heart; I won't let anything happen to you."

Fiend at My Door

Shari whimpered full of anxiety, "It's okay, baby."

Bobby hastily climbed over the banister. Shari lifted Alyssa and carefully placed her on Bobby's back. He climbed down safely to the ground. Shari lovingly looked over at Amber. "Come on baby, your next."

Shari helped Amber over the railing. Amber climbed down the rope like a spider perfectly crawls down its web. Shari climbed down right after her. Then Kelli hurried down the sheets. Next was Ashley. Liz quickly followed.

Katherine shook like a leaf in a storm. Her eyes were dilated and her breathing was erratic. She continually bit her nails as she waited for her turn to climb down. As soon she saw Liz was on the ground, she anxiously climbed over the banister and scuttled down to safety.

The thumps were increasing and so was the crack in the glass.

Bobby and Maxwell yelled up toward the balcony. "Come on, Nora, hurry up!"

Fiend at My Door

Nora heard the sound of the crashing glass. Her voice was full of fear. She screamed at the crew, "Run!"

Maxwell and Bobby watched with great foreboding as she untied the makeshift rope.

Bobby yelled up toward the balcony, "No, Nora, don't do this!"

She looked down at Bobby with heart-ache. She blew him a kiss goodbye. Bobby and Maxwell watched in complete horror as the blood suckers attacked her like a mad mob. It looked like something straight out of a horror movie. In no time at all, the ugly ghouls were enjoying her warm tasty flesh. It was gut-wrenching to watch the vile creatures tear into her flesh. The ugly ghouls devoured her piecemeal. Bobby and Maxwell could see the creatures' sharp fangs rip into her arms and neck. It was a horrific sight. Bobby stood stiff with grief. He looked solemn. His eyes were full of tears. He wept for the loss of his friend.

Maxwell nudged Bobby on the shoulder. Disheartened he said, "Come on, there is nothing we can do for her."

Fiend at My Door

The remaining crew ran with the speed of lightening toward Maxwell's vehicle. But before they could reach it, they were caught off guard by several ghouls. The children screamed and cried aloud with terror.

Kelli was confronted by one. She fought off the zombie with all her might. There was no way she was going to allow this flesh eating zombie to get her child. She had already lost her husband to the blood lust creatures, and she had no plans on losing her daughter too. She ordered Amber, "Stay close to me."

Bobby rushed to help Wes protect Kyle and Alyssa. He may have been a bit of a coward but he grew a set of balls and rushed in for the attack. The last thing he wanted on his conscience was that he allowed innocent children to get killed, especially if he could have done something.

Katherine was petrified. She squealed at the sight of the blood thirsty hulk approaching her full throttle. Quick thinking, she took off one of her four inch high-heel shoes. She raised her hand high and swung down hard. She managed to clobber the hellion in the head. The heel of her shoe left a deep gash in the succubus brain. But before she could turn around and make a run for it, another ghoul grabbed her from behind and took a deep bite out of her scrawny neck.

Before Ashley knew what hit her, she was surrounded by three hellions. One of the demons jumped on her back. The other two quickly helped to pull her down to the ground. She kicked and screamed at the succubus. She never had a chance. She was out numbered and soon the wretched creatures swarmed over her and she disappeared in a mist of red and bloody meat.

Maxwell was busy fighting his own battle. When he looked over and saw Ashley on the ground, his adrenaline kicked into high gear. He gave the ghoul a mighty upper cup and then raced over to help Ashley fight off the fiends, but it was too late. The bloodsuckers managed to bite a good chunk out of Ashley's arm and stomach. They pulled her guts out and sucked down her intestines. Maxwell watched in terror as the hellions stuck out their long tongues and licked their bloody lips with satisfaction. He had no choice but to retreat. He looked over and saw that his sister and niece were also in need of help. He rushed to their aide. He and his sister fought vigorously to get the crazed ghouls off of them. Maxwell quickly grabbed a hold of Amber and swept her into his arms. He and his sister ran with all their might toward his car.

Bobby held Alyssa tightly in his arms. He sprinted toward safety. By the time he reached the vehicle he was gasping for air. He was still in a daze. He could not stop picturing Nora's sacrifice. He knew he would never have the guts to be that selfless.

The remaining survivors hurriedly gathered into the SUV. Maxwell plunged down hard on the accelerator. He drove like a maniac to escape the horrors behind him. All during the drive, he continually envisioned the blood suckers eating Ashley alive. He could not stop picturing how they viciously ripped her apart and ate her insides like some type of tasty dessert. They sucked up her intestines like kids suck up spaghetti noodles. He wept from the horror and monstrous acts that were taking place only a few miles behind him.

Wes sat breathlessly on the passenger side. His heart thumped hard against his chest. Sweat dripped off his forehead. He tried desperately to catch his breath. He felt terrible about Nora, Katherine and Ashley, but he was grateful that his family was still in tact. He looked back at his children's terrorized faces. All he could think was 'how in the hell can this be happening?' He presented his family with an apprehensive, yet relieved smile.

Liz was silent. She kept thinking about Johnny. She wondered if the starved crazed zombies had gotten to him. She thought about what Johnny told her about Doctor Gunter. *'Where was the good doctor? Did he knowingly plan the mass destruction that was taking place? Why had he not shown up at the hotel to help Johnny?'* Nothing made any sense.

The Embassy

The car was filled with solemn hearts and sobbing disbelief. After several miles of driving like the devil was hot on his heels, Maxwell abruptly stopped the vehicle. He was incapable of going any further. His heart was heavy and his eyes were clouded with tears. Unable to keep his inner pain hidden any longer, he violently banged his hands on the steering wheel and screamed aloud with anguish, "Why is this happening?"

Wes completely understood his pain. Sympathetic to Maxwell's grief, he humbly suggested, "Hey, let me drive.

Maxwell wiped his tears away and somberly stepped out of the car. Weak and tired, he stumbled over to the passenger side. Dispirited, he climbed into the vehicle. Kelli reached over and gently patted his shoulder. Maxwell was disappointed that he allowed himself to fall apart. He wanted and needed to be strong for his sister and niece.

Wes drove full of fear and uncertainty of his family's fate down the dark, unpaved road. However, the more distance he put between them and the blood suckers, the safer he felt.

"No one is ever going to believe this," Liz said.

"Once they go back to the hotel they will become believers pretty freaking quick," Bobby added bitterly.

Suddenly there was a loud burst. The car skidded out of control. Wes fought hard to keep his grip on the steering wheel to try to keep the SUV from tumbling over.

"What the hell!" Maxwell shouted.

"Please, no God," Shari screeched. She gripped Alyssa and Kyle closer to her body.

The vehicle slid about. Eventually, Wes was able to regain control. He stopped the car in the middle of the road. He and Maxwell hurriedly leaped out of the vehicle.

Maxwell grabbed the sides of his head. He could not believe their bad luck. "Hell no, this can't be happening!"

Shari rolled down the car window and shouted out, "What's going on?"

"We have a flat," Wes shouted back.

"Give me a break," Bobby murmured.

The Embassy

Kelli remained silent. Although her crying stopped, she still looked dazed and confused. She took hold of Amber's hand and held it tightly.

Amber looked lost. She could not believe that her father was gone. She silently prayed that God would not take her mother and uncle as well.

Liz got out of the car. She walked around the vehicle. The look on her face was glum. "Crap, we are never going to make it on this."

Wes and Maxwell walked around the vehicle. Neither man could believe their eyes. The car had three blow outs.

"How can this be?" Maxwell remarked.

Bobby leaned his head out the window and shouted, "What's going on?"

"Just sit tight," Wes yelled back.

Liz nervously looked about the vast darkness. Skeptical, she walked over to Maxwell and Wes. Her voice was low. She looked spooked. She rubbed her cold arms up and down. Her eyes large she said, "This is no accident."

The Embassy

"Who would do something like this?" Maxwell grunted.

Bobby eventually got out of the car. He walked over to the group. Once he noticed the flat tires, He knew instantly that they were in deep trouble.

"What now?" Liz asked.

Gravely, Wes said, "We have no choice. We have to continue on foot."

Kelli looked at her daughter's frightened face. Meekly she said, "I need you to stay here. I will be right back."

Amber whimpered, "Don't leave me, Mommy."

Kelli's voice was soft, "I promise I am not going far. I just need to talk to your Uncle Max."

"I'll stay here with the kids," Shari added.

Kelli kissed the top of her daughter's forehead and slowly climbed out of the vehicle. She walked over toward the group. Her voice was full of despair. After analyzing their current situation, despondent she asked her brother, "What are we going to do now?"

The Embassy

Maxwell took her to the side. He kept his tone low. "We have to go the rest of the way on foot."

"Tell me this isn't happening," she whimpered.

"Just be cool, Kelli. We will get through this and be home before you know it."

Kelli looked into her brother's eyes. She knew he was trying to be strong for her, but she also knew he was just as scared as she was. She did not want to put any more pressure on him, especially considering he had lost Ashley to the zombies. She shook her head up and down, "Okay, whatever we have to do to get home."

Shari continued to stare out the window at the group. She was anxious to find out what was going on. She shouted out the window, "What's going on over there?"

Wes somberly walked over to her window. He looked distressed. "We are going to have to go the rest of the way on foot. Three of the tires are blown out."

Eyes bucked, she said with astonishment, "You have to be kidding?"

"Just sit tight," Wes ordered.

The Embassy

Shari was full of concern for the safety of her family. She hugged her children even tighter. She looked at Amber's frightened face. She tried hard to hide her own fears. She displayed a pleasant smile and said, "It's going to be alright, baby. We are going to get out of here." Shari's eyes roamed around the darkness fretfully. She was petrified of what may be lurking within the shadows of the night.

Wes walked over to the group. "We can't wait around here." He looked at Maxwell and asked, "Do you have any flash-lights?"

"Yeah, I have a couple in the trunk."

They all walked over to the car. Maxwell popped open the hatch and pulled forward the toolbox.

It did not take long before Bobby's cynical attitude resurfaced. "Why don't we all take a number to see who gets killed next?"

Grief stricken and angry, Maxwell turned around and rushed upon him. He had a firm grip around Bobby's neck. His face was mean and his tone was brutal. "I have had about enough of your crap!"

Wes pulled Maxwell off of Bobby. His voice was loud, "Let's calm down. We are all in this together."

Bobby rubbed his hurt neck, turned around and walked back to the car's side entrance.

"Come on. We're wasting time," Liz said.

Kelli looked at her brother with empathy. She knew he was just as devastated by the death of Ashley as she was for her be-loved Michael.

When Bobby returned to the car, Shari quickly asked, "What's going on?"

Glib, Bobby answered, "We're all doomed."

Wes walked over to Shari's window. He looked defeated. "Gather the kids. It's time to go."

Shari could feel her heart sink. She stared into her husband's bleak eyes. Then she looked at the frightened children. For a split second she thought, 'How could a peaceful family vacation in the country turn into such a nightmare?' She listlessly climbed out of the car. Kyle hopped out behind her. Wes took Alyssa into his arms. Kelli walked over and opened the door for Amber. They walked around to the back of the vehicle to join the others.

Maxwell held out a flashlight to Wes and he gave one to Kelli. Bobby squeezed between them and grabbed a hammer out the toolbox. Maxwell released a sigh of annoyance. Wes reached over and grabbed a couple screwdrivers. He handed one to Shari and one to Liz. Shari remained quiet, but the look on her face showed defeat.

Wes could tell by the look on his wife's face that she felt all was hopeless. He tried to reassure her, "We are going to get through this," he said.

The group stayed close together. They were silent as they walked down the lonely, dark unpaved road. You could hear their swallows and breathing. Maxwell thought for sure that the group could hear the sound of his heart thumping against his chest.

The Embassy

Amber looked up at her uncle and asked, "Uncle Max, do you think we are going to make it back home?"

There was no way he could tell her his true feelings. He displayed a confident grin and said, "Uncle Max is not going to let anything happen to you or your mommy. Yes, I am sure we will make it back home. And when we get there Trevor will be waiting at the door for you."

The picture of her sweet puppy waiting to be rubbed put a tiny smile on Amber's innocent face.

Out of nowhere a shiny bright light flashed in their faces. A gruff voice shouted out, "Stop! Don't go any further!"

Before they knew what hit them, they were confronted by men in uniforms. It appeared the men were from the military based on how they were dressed. There was a sense of relief amongst the group.

Bobby sighed loudly with relief, "Thank God."

"Who are you?" one of the officers asked.

The Embassy

Wes stepped forward with Alyssa in his arms. He spoke fast, "I'm Wes. We were attacked back at the hotel. You have to get help out there!"

"We are taking care of that." The officer looked at the group and asked, "Is this all of you?"

Maxwell stepped forward. He pointed his finger behind him and frantically demanded, "You need to do something. The people at the hotel need help!"

A few of the other soldiers walked forward toting guns.

The officer asked coldly, "Have any of you been bitten?"

"No, we are all fine," Wes answered.

The officer ordered, "Come with us. We have a small camp ground just up the road."

Bobby eagerly ran forward and followed behind the soldiers like a well trained puppy. Liz walked between Shari and Kelli. Kyle stayed close by his father's side. Maxwell was close behind them holding Amber's hand tightly.

Liz muttered to Shari and Kelli, "Doesn't this all seem a bit odd to you?"

Keeping her voice equally low, Kelli asked, "What do you mean?"

"For starters, where are all the police? Why are they hiding out in the dark? And what the heck happened to the car?"

"Let's just be thankful that someone found us," Shari remarked.

They walked a short distance before they reached the military jeeps. They all climbed inside the vehicles. They were driven to a location that looked like an abandoned walk-in clinic.

"Where are we?" Wes immediately inquired.

The leading officer jumped out the jeep. "This is our temporary headquarters. Please, follow me." He could tell from the uncertain look in their eyes that they were reluctant to follow his orders. "It's safe here," the officer reassured them.

Everyone climbed out the jeeps. Their eyes were wide with fear just waiting on the blood suckers to jump from out the bushes and pounce. Once they were all inside the facility, the officer led them to a large room where cots were positioned against the far back wall.

Bobby briskly walked over to one of the cots and plopped down. He exhaled a breath of relief, wiped his sweaty forehead and mumbled, "Thank God."

The commanding officer grinned. "Yes, I am sure you all must be exhausted." He then looked at the ladies. He pointed his finger, "The restrooms are just down the hall."

Wes walked over to the cots. He placed Alyssa's tired body down. Kyle sat beside his sister. Wes patted Kyle on the top of his head.

"I'm proud of you, son. Now just stay here with your sister."

Amber was reluctant to leave her mother. She squeezed her mother's hand tightly.

Kelli looked down at her distraught daughter. She tried her best to sound confi- dent. "Its okay, Amber, we're safe now. Just go have a seat next to Kyle and I promise I will be right back."

The frightened child looked over at Kyle and Alyssa. She slowly turned around and followed her mother's orders.

The Embassy

Shari, Liz and Kelli walked down the dim-ly lit hall to the restroom. Liz felt unnerved by the officer standing guard. Although she knew it was standard procedure, something felt wrong to her about the whole thing. She continued to think back to Johnny. When she and the ladies entered the restroom, she quickly turned to them. She looked spooked. Her voice was extremely low and her eyes were enflamed. "Something isn't right here!" she exclaimed.

Worried, Shari asked, "What do you mean?"

Liz walked over to the stalls. She bent down and checked them all out for any unwanted guests or prying ears. Shari and Kelli stood by looking baffled and concerned. Liz walked back over to them and grabbed a hold of their hands. She walked them over to the sink. She turned on the faucet and just let the water run to drown out the sound of her voice.

Scared, Kelli asked, "What's going on with you?"

Liz whispered, "I think the officers are in on this?"

Shari looked puzzled, "What? Why would you think that?"

"Shih," Liz said with panic. She continued to explain, "I have a friend named Johnny. He told me that he was receiving these experimental shots from a doctor named Gunter."

Kelli interrupted, "I don't see what that has to do with what's going on."

"Just listen," Liz grunted. "Johnny was the cook at the hotel. He told me that he cut his finger and he believed his blood dripped into the food."

Shari and Kelli's face turned pale. Putting two and two together, they quickly realized that the food was infected.

Liz looked almost deranged. She looked deeply into their eyes and said, "Did you see the name on the officer's shirt? It said Gunter!"

You could see the light come on in Kelli and Shari's head. Now they were also worried.

"We have to tell the others," Shari mumbled.

"I know, but we don't want them to know that we suspect them," Liz said.

The Embassy

"Why is this happening?" Kelli whimpered.

Neither woman had an answer for the horrific ordeal that was taking place. There was no sane or rational explanation to justify the heinous events taking place at the Embassy.

There was a knock on the restroom door. "Are you ladies alright in there?"

All three of the women nearly jumped out of their skin.

Liz shouted back, "We're fine. We will be out in a minute."

Shari and Kelli looked terrified. They splattered some cold water on their face and sucked in a deep breath before leaving the restroom. When they rejoined the men, Wes immediately noticed the strange look in his wife's eyes.

Gunter spread out his hand toward the women and said, "Come, have a seat."

The women took a seat at the long metal table. There was bread, meat, cheese, wine and fruit spread out. Although all were famished, they were reluctant to eat the goodies.

Gunter displayed a wide grin, "Dig in, dig in." He realized the group was scared to eat the food. He reached over, grabbed some meat and cheese and swallowed it down. Once he ate, the others decided it was safe to enjoy the meal.

"What are those things?" Maxwell asked.

"We're not quite sure."

Suspicious, Liz asked, "How did you know what was happening?"

Gunter filled his glass with some red wine. He took a large swallow. "We received a distress call before all the lines went dead."

Liz was anxious to tell the men what she believed was transpiring. She continued to question Gunter. "What about the other's at the hotel?"

Gunter broke apart a piece of bread. He spread a healthy serving of jam on it and shoved it in his mouth. "Rest assured that we are doing everything possible to help any remaining survivors." He stood up and rubbed his belly. "Why don't all of you try to get some rest? We will head out first thing in the morning."

Wes displayed a grateful grin. "Thank you."

Gunter turned and left the room.

Wes walked over to Shari. Worried, he asked, "Are you alright?"

Liz rose up from the table and took Maxwell by the hand. She put her finger on her lips. Bobby looked on with curiosity. He quickly joined them.

"What's up?" Maxwell asked.

"It's Gunter," Liz whispered.

"What about him?" Bobby squealed.

Shari and Wes walked over to the group.

Liz began to explain. She looked scared. "I left my friend Johnny back at the hotel. He told me that he was receiving some experimental drugs from non-other than Officer Gunter."

Maxwell interrupted, "Wait, just hold on. How do we know these two men are one in the same?"

Liz looked astounded by his comment. Tight lipped, she said, "Do you really think it is a coincidence that those officers were out in the middle of nowhere and that the officer who rescued us name just happens to be Gunter?" She continued to vent her frustration, "Hell, it's not like Gunter is a common name like Jones or Smith."

"Let's all try to keep a cool head," Wes said.

Liz calmed down. She continued with her story. "Anyway, Johnny told me that he cut his finger."

Bobby rudely interrupted, "Who gives a crap about your friend's cut finger?"

Liz looked mean. Her teeth were clinched, "If you would shut up and listen. Johnny was the cook at the hotel. His blood infected the food."

"I'll be damned," Maxwell muttered, "We're all doomed."

"I don't think so," Liz stated. "I mean think about it. If we were going to change into one of those freaks, we would have done it by now."

"She's right," Wes agreed.

"What do we do now?" Kelli asked.

"For one, we play dumb. We don't want them to know we are on to them."

Maxwell paced around fretfully. "We need to get the hell out of here."

Sarcastically, Bobby retorted, "If what Liz said is true, they are not going to just let us walk out the front door."

Upset and grieving, Maxwell rushed upon Bobby and yelled, "I have had just about enough of you."

Wes jumped between the men and held Maxwell back. "Hey, we have to keep a level head."

Gunter entered the room. "Is everything okay in here?"

"We're fine. Just a little on edge," Wes said.

"Like I said, you have nothing to worry about. My men are standing guard. Nothing will get past them."

The ladies presented apprehensive smiles. Bobby looked like a scared rat. Both Wes and Maxwell merely grinned politely at the officer. Gunter turned around and left the room.

The Embassy

"Come on and sit down," Wes suggested to Shari.

Shari looked so over-wrought. She sat on the small cot beside the children.

Wes walked back over to the group. They huddled in a circle. Wes explained, "We all need some rest. We will have to take turns standing guard."

Maxwell looked grief-stricken and tired. His eyes were cloudy. He could not help but picture Ashley's cheerful smile. Then he envisioned the horror of her face as the blood suckers ripped her apart and ate her alive. He could not fathom how any of this could possibly be happening. He reached into his pants pocket and pulled out a small box. Everyone seemed to be focused on him.

He muttered though his tears, "I was going to ask Ashley to marry me." He opened the small black velvet box and displayed the shiny diamond ring. He broke down with pain. "Why is this happening?"

Kelli quickly walked over to her brother and wrapped her arms around him. Although he tried to be strong, he sobbed hard with sorrow. Kelli also wept for the loss of Ashley and her dear husband, Michael.

Maxwell's pain made Bobby's emerge. Once again, Bobby found himself thinking of Nora. He regretted that he never would have the chance to tell her of his true feelings. Nora died a terrible death not knowing how much he really loved her.

Maxwell abruptly stopped crying. He stepped back and looked deeply into his sister's caring eyes. He knew he needed to be strong for the both of them. "I'm sorry. We don't have time for this." He somberly walked away and glared out the window into the darkness. All were full of despair, fear and confusion.

Wes looked over at his wife and the kids. He was more determined than ever to get his family out of this hellish nightmare.

Alyssa had finally awakened. She looked so tiny and scared. All she could do was look into her mother's eyes with pain. Shari tenderly stroked the side of her daughter's frightened face.

"You need to eat," she said caringly to her daughter. Shari walked over to the table and gathered up some of the food for the children.

Wes continued to stare at her with love and concern. He looked over at Maxwell, who remained stiff as a mannequin staring out the window into the vast darkness.

Bobby commented, "I counted and there are only ten of them."

Wes turned to look at him. He asked, "Do you have a plan?"

Hopeful, Bobby replied, "I say if we can get Gunter and take him as our hostage, they will be forced to let us go."

Wes considered the idea. He said, "It's possible."

Liz quickly shot their plan down. "I seriously doubt they are going to let us go. Gunter doesn't want his little secret exposed."

Wes gazed at her. He hated to admit it but he knew she was right. 'They had to do something but what?' He pondered.

All of a sudden Maxwell frantically stumbled back from the window. His eyes grew wide. He looked like he had come face to face with the devil. He pointed his trembling finger toward the window and shouted, "They're coming!"

Everyone panicked. Wes, Liz and Bobby saw the blood suckers fast approaching out of the bushes. Gun shots blazed! Wes raced over to the children. He snatched up Alyssa. Maxwell rushed over and grabbed Amber. The group frantically ran down the hall, dazed and scared beyond reason.

One of the guards burst into the building. He yelled and waved his hand, "This way!"

The frantic group followed behind him. The soldier shot several of the ghouls in the head as they ran down the hall. "Come on, hurry up!" he ordered.

Two of the hellions were fast approaching Bobby. He cried out like a little girl, "Help! Help me!"

Wes instantly handed Alyssa to Shari. He turned around and went to Bobby's aid. The officer continued to unload rounds of bullets into the oncoming blood suckers.

Maxwell noticed that Bobby and Wes were in a jam. He ordered Amber to go to

Kelli. He turned around and swiftly ran down the hall to help Bobby and Wes fight off the ghouls. The men were barely able to fight off the creatures. The men fought their way through and fretfully ran down the hall and joined the others. They came upon a steel door. The officer quickly handed his weapon to Wes. He punched in his pass code and the door opened.

"Come on, get inside!" the officer ordered.

As soon as they were all safely in the room, Wes jumped in the officers' face and grabbed him by his uniformed shirt. Wes looked ferocious. He yelled at the top of his lungs, "Tell us what the hell is gong on here?"

The officer appeared just a shook up as everyone else. He peered around the small room at all the terrified and befuddled faces. He seemed fixated on Alyssa's tiny frightened face.

Maxwell could not take anymore. He stormed toward the officer. Angered, he shoved Wes aside. He grabbed the officer by the collar. His hands gripped the officer's neck tightly. He shoved the officer back against the wall. Viciously, he shouted, "What the hell are those things?"

The officer could barely breathe. Wes intervened. "Calm down, Maxwell. We all want answers."

Unwillingly, Maxwell released the officer. He angrily stumped off toward his sister and niece grunting with anger, fear and confusion. "Shit, what in the hell is going on?"

Meanwhile, Shari covered Alyssa's ears. The blood suckers clawed at the door. They made the most sickening hissing sounds. Their scratches sound like nails against a chalkboard and their hissing sound like cold winds whistling through trees.

Kyle tried to be as strong as his dad. He grabbed hold of Alyssa's small hand and told his mother. "I got her, Mom."

For once, Bobby elected to remain silent. He was petrified by the thoughts of how close he came to being eaten alive. He stood stiff, silently thanking God that he was not the blood thirsty ghoul's next meal.

Kelli held her daughter's hand tightly. She promised, "It's going to be alright, baby. We are going to get out of here."

The Embassy

Wes looked angrily at the officer. He tugged the officer's badge. "Office Stein is it?" He yelled, "Start talking."

Officer Stein slowly began to unfold the mystery behind the transformation of the blood crazed ghouls. His voice was eerie as he explained, "It all started a few months ago. Doctor Gunter lost his five year old daughter due to a rare blood disease. He was devastated by her death." Officer Stein's eyes were glum. "He had lost her mother when she was born due to the same rare blood disorder."

The group remained silent and stoic. They were desperate for answers.

Stein continued, "Doctor Gunter was a scientist. He was determined to bring his daughter back. He had been working on a stop secret serum to bring back the dead." He looked around the room at all the scared faces and continued with his tale. "He purchased this building and began experimenting on human Guinea pigs."

"That doesn't make any sense," Kelli remarked. "Even if he could bring back the dead, his daughter's body would be rotted in six feet of dirt."

Officer Stein walked over to a freezer and opened it. All stood still, sickened and appalled by the sight of Gunter's daughter's frozen body.

Kelli put her hand over her mouth. She felt ill to her stomach. "That's sick," she said with disgust.

"I told you, he was desperate," Officer Stein commented.

Liz immediately thought about Johnny. She now understood what injections Johnny received from the doctor.

Officer Stein continued with his tale of gore. "He had a few college kids volunteer for the program. Of course they had no clue what they were really signing up for. He sold the young kids a bill of goods. He told them that the injections were to make them more energetic and increase their memory. But they were unable to withstand the side effects. Only one of his volunteers made it through the program."

The Embassy

Liz glumly said aloud, "Johnny?"

Shamefully, Officer Stein admitted, "Yes, Johnny Rickens was the only one who successfully completed the process."

Maxwell was so incensed, his voice vibrated. "Exactly what process was that?"

Stein confessed with disgrace, "The process of dying and being brought back to life."

Liz looked astounded. "You mean to tell me that Johnny is dead?"

"Not dead," Stein explained, "But dead-alive."

Kelli shivered. "What type of madness is that? You're sick!"

"Doctor Gunter was desperate. All that mattered to him was bringing back his daughter. We are still unsure how all this happened. All I know is that Johnny telephoned Gunter and told him he was not feeling well. Gunter called me and a few of his close comrades. By the time we made it to the Embassy, it was too late. People were running scared and being eaten alive."

The Embassy

Angrily, Shari glared at him and grunted through clinched teeth, "So you just left us there to die!"

Shame-faced he admitted, "Gunter was afraid to let his secret out. He decided to distance himself from the problem. He figured once everyone turned, there would be no one left to tell about his little project."

With the truth exposed, Maxwell pointed at Officer Stein and shouted, "So you were not out in the woods hoping to rescue any survivors, you were out there waiting to kill anyone who had not turned into one of those freaks!"

The officer lowered his head in ignominy.

"I'll be damned," Bobby mumbled.

There was nothing but hate in Shari's eyes. She yelled, "Now what?"

"Doctor Gunter was eaten by his own creation. All I can do now is try to get us out of here alive."

Embittered, Wes asked, "Do you have a phone or any way to communicate with the outside world?"

The Embassy

"It's in my truck."

Liz looked over at Bobby. Sullenly she remarked, "Well, Bobby, I guess you got your wish."

Bobby looked stupefied.

She looked defeated and said, "You're back in the closet." She slumped down on the hard metal chair full of despair.

Wes looked all around the room. "Is there another way out of here?" he asked the officer.

Stein pointed up toward the air duct.

"Where does it lead?" Maxwell asked.

"It leads to a room at the back of the building."

Worried, Wes asked, "How far is that from the jeeps?"

"There are some jeeps located at the back door of the room," he said.

Wes tried to come up with a plan. "What we need is someone to back the jeep up to the back door."

The officer took Wes' lead. "I can cover for one of you."

Everyone was beyond shocked when Bobby volunteered. He stood up strong. It was as if he took a sip of courage juice. His chest was tight and his tone was full of confidence. "I can do it. I use to run track. I am pretty damn fast." He noticed how everyone looked at him with doubt. He was unyielding. "Seriously, I can do it."

"Where are the keys?" Maxwell asked.

"The keys are in the vehicles."

Everyone looked at each other. Their options were limited. They realized that trying to get to the jeep was their best option.

In a military fashion, the officer took charge. He gripped his rifle and yelled, "Let's move it."

Bobby was lifted up first into the air duct. He reached down his hand and pulled up Kyle. Then the women went up. Wes lifted Alyssa up to Shari and then he lift Amber up to her. Wes followed. Maxwell went next. The officer held up his weapon to Maxwell. He jumped up and entered the shaft. They frightfully crawled through the tight hot shaft.

When they made it to the end, Bobby cautiously opened the vent. He lowered his head and looked inside the room. He looked back at the group and whispered, "It's clear.

He jumped down. He saw a desk near the corner. Thinking quickly, he pushed the desk under the shaft. He stood on it and helped the women and children down.

Once everyone was safely in the room, they remained silent with fear. The men crawled over to the small window. Officer Stein stooped up just a bit and cautiously peered out the glass.

"What do you see?" Wes whispered.

"I counted at least twelve of them."

"It might as well be a hundred," Bobby muttered.

"How much ammo do you have left?" Maxwell asked.

The officer looked at his weapon and pulled out the clip. "I've got about half a clip left."

Wes presented a stern expression when he told Bobby. "You had better be damn fast."

Bobby looked every bit the scared nerd. "I can do it."

The Embassy

Officer Stein instructed the group, "Once he backs the jeep up to the door, we have to be swift and ready to go."

Wes turned to his son and ordered, "Stay close."

Alyssa cried, "I don't want to die, Mommy."

Shari cradled Alyssa in her arms. She tenderly stroked her daughter's blonde hair. "It's going to be alright, baby. We are going to get out of this."

Kelli hugged Amber tightly and whispered, "We are going to be home before you know it."

Amber looked into her mother's haunted eyes. She feared this was the last she would ever see her. Lovingly, she said, "I love you, Mom."

"I love you too, baby," Kelli replied with a soft and gentle tone. Then Kelli looked over at her brother as though she would never see him again. Her eyes were flooded with tears. She moved her lips with a silent, "I love you, Max."

The Embassy

He whispered back, "I love you too, Sis."

Maxwell turned to Bobby. Sternly, he asked, "are you ready?'

Bobby put up a strong front. "Ready as I will ever be."

Everyone stood back away from the door, except Officer Stein and Maxwell. Stein looked at Bobby. He held his hand up and stretched out his fingers. "On the count of three," He let down one finger at a time and counted, "One, two, three!"

Maxwell quickly opened the door. Bobby took off like a sprinter. Officer Stein did not waste any time unloading his rounds of am-munition into the ghouls. They were coming fast.

Alyssa screamed, "No, Mommy, don't let them get me!"

Bobby had made it safely to the jeep. He started the engine and quickly backed up the vehicle to the back door.

There was a sense of urgency amongst the group. Officer Stein yelled at them, "Hurry! Get in."

The Embassy

The group was fast on their feet. They hurriedly raced toward the jeep and gathered inside for safety.

The bloodsuckers seemed to be coming from all angles. They leaped out of the bushes and bum-rushed Officer Stein. Before he climbed into the jeep, he was out of bullets. He yelled at Bobby, "Go! Damn it, get out of here!"

Several of the blood suckers pulled Stein down on the ground. Their sharp claws dug into his flesh and ripped him apart. His screams were gut-wrenching. The blood

starved monsters looked like a pack of canni-
bals enjoying a long awaited feast.

Shari and Kelli were thinking alike. They
placed their hands over their daughter's eyes
in order to shield them from witnessing the
horrific scene.

Bobby drove like a NASCAR racer. He
plunged on the accelerator and fled from the
man eating killers. He drove for a straight hour
without saying a word looking completely
insane. His eyes were enlarged, his mouth
hung open and he gripped the steering wheel
so tightly that the palms of his hands were red.

The Embassy

Without warning he began to slow down. Everyone panicked. He pointed ahead. Excitedly, he yelled, "Look, it's a gas station!"

Wes was hesitant. "Just hold on, Bobby, we don't know how far this disease has spread."

"He's right," Maxwell said.

Bobby slowed the vehicle and drove up to the gas pump with great trepidation.

The friendly attendant came right out. With a Southern twang and a bright smile, he asked, "What can I do ya for?"

There was a sense of relief amongst them all. Nothing appeared to be out of the norm.

Wes talked fast. "Do you have a phone?

"Sure do. It's just inside on the wall to your left."

Wes hopped out of the vehicle and walked fast to the entrance. When he entered the station, he looked about hastily for the phone. Just as the attendant instructed, the phone was on the left side of the wall. He hurried over to it. He snatched up the receiver and immediately dialed 911.

Bobby hopped out of the Jeep and began to pump the gas.

In his country twang, the attendant asked Bobby, "You guys coming from the hotel?"

Bobby looked at him strangely. "Yes, why do you ask?"

"I had a guy show up here from the ho-tel. He looked sick. Said he believed it was food poisoning."

Bobby was immediately alarmed, "Where is he now?"

"He went into the bathroom. He hasn't come out yet."

Bobby nervously pulled out a twenty dollar bill and handed it to the attendant. Then he hurriedly closed the cap on the gas tank of the jeep. He jumped in the jeep and frantically told Maxwell, "We need to go!"

Nervously, Maxwell asked, "What's up?"

Panicked Bobby said, "Get Wes now!"

Maxwell did not need to ask anymore questions. On pure reflex, he leaped out the jeep and ran toward the gas station entrance, yelling out as he ran, "Wes, get out of there!"

Bobby sped the jeep up near the doors' entrance. The attendant looked dumbfounded. He did not understand their anxiousness. He muttered under his breath, "City folks, they're always in a rush to go nowhere."

Wes slowly turned his head. He heard someone coming from out the bathroom. He dropped the receiver and attempted to run, but the oversized goon was quick and strong. Wes didn't stand a chance. The giant grabbed him in a tight grip and started to enjoy his warm flesh.

Maxwell entered the gas station. He took a step back. His heart felt as thought it stopped beating. He was mortified by the sight of the goon devouring Wes. Traumatized, he stared and stood stiffly as he watched the ghoul take a mighty bite out of Wes' neck. For a split second, Maxwell was immobile. It all seemed like a bad horror movie. Unfortunately, it was all too real. He realized that it was too late to do anything to help Wes. He had no choice but to retreat. Maxwell, full of heartache, turned around and ran back to the jeep.

Shari screamed with terror, "No, Wes! No!"

Liz and Kelli hugged the children.

Kyle fought with Liz to be released from her tight grip. "Let me go, let me go," he demanded. "I need to help my dad."

Liz was strong and she managed to keep a firm grip on the child.

Kyle cried out for his father, "Daddy!"

Maxwell jumped back in the jeep. He screamed at Bobby, eyes wild with fear, "Go! We can't help him now. Get out of here!"

Bobby put the jeep in reverse and zoomed backward. All witnessed the large ghoul come out of the gas station and chase down the attendant. It was horrific. They watched the creature take a big plug out of the attendant's arm. The chubby old man screamed violently. The poor man tried to put up a fight but it was useless. Soon, the over-sized ghoul had pulled the attendant down to the ground. He opened his large mouth and displayed his blade like teeth. He lowered his head and took a chunk out of the attendant's neck. Blood was everywhere. The demon licked his lips with pleasure and displayed a wide smile of satisfaction. Then he plunged his hands into the attendant's belly and pulled out his guts. He sucked down his intestines like sucking up juice through a straw.

Shari looked upon the gruesome scene with anguish. When she looked over at the gas station door, she saw Wes stumble out. She screamed out, "Wes......!"

Alyssa cried out, "Daddy, Daddy!"

Wes was bleeding profusely. It appeared from the crazed look in his eyes that he was already turning into one of the crazed blood suckers.

Maxwell was speechless.

"My God, how many more are there?" Kelli screeched.

The few survivors feared their destiny. There was no way of knowing how many more people left the hotel and made it back to the city before their sick lust for human flesh consumed them.

City of Doom

Bobby drove like a bat out of hell. Mental pictures of Wes being devoured by the blood crazed ghoul consumed his every thought. Again, he found himself thinking of Nora. He muttered through his disbelief, "Let this be a dream. It's just a bad dream." He continued to rant, "This is just a bad version of the Wizard of Oz. I am going to wake back up in my warm bed. God, let this just be a terrible dream."

Shari was inconsolable. She sobbed uncontrollably all the while she held on tightly to Alyssa. Images of Wes stumbling out of the gas station all bloody and thirsting for blood filled her mind. "Why damn it? Why?" were the only words that emitted from her quivering lips.

Kyle was also devastated by the loss of his father. He suddenly felt a sense of responsibility. He refused to cry because he felt that he needed to be strong for his mother and sister. He took his mother's hand. Bravely, he said, "It's going to be alright, Mom. I will take care of you."

Shari stared bleakly into her son's eyes. She knew he was trying his best to step into his father's shoes. She felt nothing but pity for herself and her children. *'How would they ever survive without Wes?'*

Maxwell felt such a sense of loss. He thought *'if it were not for Wes' kindness, he, his sister and Amber would be dead by now. Wes took a big chance when he opened his hotel door and allowed them entrance.'* Then he thought about Ashley and Michael having been eaten alive. '*What a horrible way to die.*

Ashley was so young and beautiful. They had

their whole lives ahead of them. How on earth

could such a gentle soul be gone?' Maxwell

admired the loving and close relationship his

sister and Michael shared. Their solid marriage

is what motivated him to want to propose

marriage to Ashley. '*Now his dream was dead*

along with the love of his life.'

Kelli hugged Amber for dear life. '*How*

could her wedding anniversary turn into such

a nightmare? How could she live without

Michael? What of Amber? The poor child

would be scarred for the rest of her life.' Then she thought about how she planned to surprise Michael with the news of her pregnancy. *'Everything was ruined. She and Amber's life would never be the same. And her unborn child will never know his father.'*

Liz was stiff with disbelief. Although she did not have much family to think of, she felt a great deal of empathy for what the others were enduring. She could only imagine their suffering and pain. She looked about the countryside. What once appeared to be beautiful scenery was now filled with gore and ugliness. The visions of flesh eating zombies would forever wreak havoc on her brain when she thought of the quaint outdoor country living.

The jeep began to slow down. Bobby leaned forward. He was relieved. "Hey, we're here!"

The rest of the crew looked ahead. There was no sign of any flesh eating crea-tures lurking about. A since of hope filled everyone's soul. Bobby continued to drive into the city. He headed for the nearest police station he could find.

"Oh, thank God," Shari said with a ray of hope.

Kelli looked into Amber's eyes. "We're almost home, baby."

Amber managed a tiny smile. She was heart sick that her father did not make it. She wondered if her pet was safe. "I can't wait to see Trevor. He must be starved," she said to her mother.

Her mother just looked at her with misty eyes and said, "I 'm sure he's fine, baby."

Maxwell remained silent. He was thankful that they were back in the city, but the demons behind him would forever be at the forefront of his mind.

Bobby pulled the vehicle up the police station. Everyone solemnly got out of the jeep. They all walked with a slow uncertain pace toward the entrance.

Once inside, Max told the women, "Stay here. Bobby and I will handle it."

The women and kids took a seat on the hard bench. Max and Bobby walked up to the front counter. Neither man knew how to even begin to explain the horrific events they narrowly escaped.

"How can I help you?" the officer asked.

Max looked at Bobby and Bobby looked at him. Max finally said, "Someone needs to get out to the Embassy right away."

Confused, the officer said, "The Embassy?"

Wound up, Bobby explained, "Yes, the Embassy. It is a hotel just north of here about two and half hours away."

Once the officer looked a little more closely, he realized that the men's clothes were disheveled and they looked distraught.

He peered away from them and looked over at the women and children seated just across the hall. He realized that something bad must have happened. They now had his full attention.

The officer pulled out a notepad. He asked, "What happened at the Embassy?"

Bobby and Max knew the officer would find their story impossible to believe, but what choice did they have?

Maxwell looked deranged. He sucked in a large breath. He tried his best to explain, "We were at the hotel and before we knew what was happening, people were eating people."

Clearly disbelieving him, the officer said, "Eating people? Right, have you been smoking? Are you gentlemen on some type of drugs?"

Maxwell was livid. He shouted, "You have to get help out there now! We barely escaped. They ate my sister's husband and they killed my girlfriend!" His voice rose, "Listen, I'm telling you; you need to get the army out there. It's a blood bath."

Bobby added, "Yeah, and they killed my friend Nora. Not to mention all the other people they killed. Please, get help out there now!"

The officer's eyes peered away from the men. He refocused his attention on the women and children. He walked from behind the counter and headed toward the women and kids. When he looked into their eyes, he saw nothing but pain and fear. Although he found it hard to believe that people were actually eating people, he knew he needed to check out their story. It was obvious that something terrible happened.

Shari looked up at the officer. Eyes bloodshot red and swollen, she cried, "They killed my husband. Please, you have to stop them."

The officer walked back over to the counter. He placed an emergency call to the Lancaster County. He explained that they needed to have some officers go to the Embassy hotel and check things out. He looked at the frightened group and said, "Don't worry; it's going to be alright. I telephoned the authorities and they are headed to check out your story. In the meantime, I need to get all the facts." He held out his hand, "Please, I need you all to come with me."

He gathered the women and children. They all followed behind him toward one of the interrogation rooms. But before they made it down the hall, all hell broke loose. The group slowly and fearfully turned their heads when they heard the sound of loud screams. When they looked back, their hearts instantly sank. The flesh eating monsters were hot on their trail.

For a brief moment the officer was immobile with incredulity. If he had not just spoken with the group, he would have sworn he was seeing things. But he knew now that their story was real. He screamed toward the group, "Hurry, follow me!"

The group fled down the hall and followed the officer to the back exit. Once again, the group was forced to run for their lives. The officer loaded the frightened passengers into a police mini-van. It was still hard for the officer to digest. But there were no longer any questions about the validity of their story. He was now witnessing the madness and chaos with his own eyes.

"What in the hell are those things?" the officer asked.

Bitterly, Maxwell grumbled, "Flesh eating zombies."

"But zombies are only in the movies," the officer remarked with a tremble in his voice.

"Somehow they found a way out of the movies and have now entered our world," Bobby gravely said.

As they fled for safety, Liz explained everything to the officer regarding Doctor Gunter's experiment gone wrong. Now the officer understood how this madness came to be. His only concern now was keeping himself and the others safe. He asked the men "Do either of you know how to shoot a gun?" He instructed them, "There are some weapons in the back. Arm yourself. It looks like we are going to be in for one hell of a ride."

The officer drove with the speed of lightning. He soon came upon a small military campground. The group did not feel safe. It looked abandoned.

"What is this place?" Kelli asked.

"It is just what it looks like. It was once used as a training camp for soldiers."

"Why did you bring us here?" Liz asked.

"Do you have a better idea? Right now, I think being as far away from people is our best bet. At least until we can figure out what the hell is going on and we can get some real help." He instructed the men. "Gather all the weapons and follow me."

The group slothfully followed behind the officer. Their only thought was, *'When will this nightmare end?'*

Maxwell thought, *'If the blood crazed ghouls managed to take over the large city, they were all doomed.'*

The group entered the abandoned building. The women and kids were exhausted. They immediately took a seat on the small twin-sized beds.

Feeling a great sense of haplessness Maxwell asked the officer, "Now what?"

"Now I call for help to get us the hell out of here."

The officer walked over to a phone that was mounted to the wall. He dialed up the military. He hastily explained the tragic and unbelievable events taking place. He reiterated the story he got from Liz regarding Doctor Gunter. He was told to sit tight. Help was on the way. He turned and looked back at the group. He was relieved to tell them, "Hey, we just need to lay low. Help should be here soon."

No one was convinced that they would make it out alive. At this point, all believed that their days were numbered. The officer turned around and headed for the outside.

Maxwell reached out his and grabbed the officer's arm. "Hey, where are you going?" he asked nervously.

"The kids look hungry. I have a small cooler full of juices and sandwiches. I'm just going to get it."

Chest heavy full of fear, Maxwell quickly suggested, "Well at least let me watch your back."

"Thanks, I appreciate that."

The officer left the building and headed for the police van to retrieve the cooler. Maxwell looked all around the perimeter. He held the rifle with a tight grip. He was ready to kill anything that moved. The two men returned to the building. The officer opened the cooler and handed the women and kids some sandwiches and cans of soda. They were grateful for the refreshments. Bobby and

Maxwell were equally grateful to have something to eat. They were all famished.

"How long before you think they will be here to rescue us?" Liz asked.

"I can't say for certain. I suppose that would depend on the madness in the city."

The group tried to relax. Eventually fatigue gave way and most of the group fell asleep on the tiny cots.

Maxwell and the officer were unable to rest. They stayed awake to stand guard.

The officer extended out his hand and said, "By the way, I'm Officer Watkins."

Max gave him a firm handshake and replied, "I'm Maxwell Grey."

The officer had a kind smile on his face when he said, "Nice to meet you, Max."

Two hours had passed. Officer Watkins and Maxwell were becoming increasingly concerned if help was truly on its way. They both jumped when they heard the sound of footsteps approaching the door. They held up their weapons ready to unload their bullets. Several militants burst in. They had their weapons up as well.

"Are you Officer Watkins?" the agent asked.

Relieved, the officer said, "Yes, and these are the people I told you about that were at the Embassy."

By this time, everyone had awakened.

"Okay, let's get all of you out of here and somewhere safe."

The group quickly gathered up and followed the commanding officer. They were placed in a military van and driven to an undisclosed facility. From there, they were placed in a chopper and flown out of the city. During their flight, the group witnessed their town being destroyed. There were fires everywhere.

"What going on down there?" Bobby asked.

The officer explained, "The disease was uncontainable. We had to destroy everything in order to prevent it from spreading."

Amber looked downward with heart-ache. She thought, *'Poor Trevor.'* She hoped that he made it to heaven with her father.

City of Doom

"My God, all of this destruction because one man could not accept the death of his daughter," Maxwell bitterly stated.

It was a horrible sight to see. Their city was destroyed and who knew how many innocent lives were destroyed with it.

Surely not everyone had turned into flesh eating zombies. Could they not work out a plan to rescue the remaining survivors? Or did no one really care to try? What was in store for them? God only knew! Shari silently thought.